ChangelingPress.com

Titan/Grease Monkey Duet

Harley Wylde

Titan/Grease Monkey Duet

Harley Wylde

All rights reserved.
Copyright ©2021 Harley Wylde

ISBN: 9798749593280

Publisher:
Changeling Press LLC
315 N. Centre St.
Martinsburg, WV 25404
ChangelingPress.com

Printed in the U.S.A.

Editor: Crystal Esau
Cover Artist: Bryan Keller

The individual stories in this anthology have been previously released in E-Book format.

No part of this publication may be reproduced or shared by any electronic or mechanical means, including but not limited to reprinting, photocopying, or digital reproduction, without prior written permission from Changeling Press LLC.

This book contains sexually explicit scenes and adult language which some may find offensive and which is not appropriate for a young audience. Changeling Press books are for sale to adults, only, as defined by the laws of the country in which you made your purchase.

Table of Contents

Titan (Hades Abyss MC 5) 4
   Prologue 5
   Chapter One..12
   Chapter Two 23
   Chapter Three...36
   Chapter Four...49
   Chapter Five 62
   Chapter Six..74
   Chapter Seven 85
   Chapter Eight..101
   Chapter Nine 112
   Chapter Ten 128
   Chapter Eleven...138
   Chapter Twelve 147
   Chapter Thirteen 160
   Epilogue 172
Titan (Hades Abyss MC 5) 175
   Deleted Scene..176
Grease Monkey -- A Bad Boy Romance 180
   Chapter One..181
   Chapter Two 191
   Chapter Three...200
   Chapter Four...214
   Chapter Five 232
   Epilogue 239
Harley Wylde..243
Changeling Press E-Books 244

Titan (Hades Abyss MC 5)
Harley Wylde

Delilah -- I love my family. I really do. But having three older brothers and an overprotective father doesn't make it easy to have a life. They've run off every guy I've ever tried to date. It's time I made a life of my own, even if that means I have to leave home to do it. I never thought I'd end up in yet another town with a motorcycle club, or that I'd be working out of their clubhouse as a webcam girl. I enjoy the freedom, and the money. No one would ever believe I'm technically a virgin. I haven't even been really, truly kissed much less done anything else with a guy before. When the club President, Titan, kissed me, then issued a challenge, how could I possibly refuse?

Titan -- I no longer looked at the girls frequenting the clubhouse the same way I had before. Being a dad changed my perspective, especially since I had a daughter. I still had fun, but it had lost its appeal. Then she walked in. Too young. Too innocent. Until she asked to join the webcam girls. The thought of strange men watching her made my hands clench. It was safer if only I had access to the feed, or so I told myself. Really, I'm just being a possessive bastard. Delilah will be mine, whether she realizes it or not. One kiss is all it takes for me to know she belongs to me. When she's taken, I know I'll do whatever it takes to get her back, and I'll bury anyone who's hurt her. Delilah is mine, and I will kill to protect her.

Prologue

Delilah

My older brother, Griffin, gave me the kind of look only your big brother could give. One that conveyed love, frustration, and a small amount of disbelief. I had to admit, I'd dropped a bomb on him. Ever since my friend Missy had moved away, I'd felt the urge to leave town and start a life elsewhere. It wasn't that I didn't love my family because I did, but my dad was overprotective, as were my three older brothers. As the baby of the family, and the only girl, I never got to have any fun.

Every single date I'd ever been on had been interrupted by one of my brothers. After a while, I'd given up on even trying. What was the point?

"You're doing what?" Griffin asked.

"I'm going to move. Missy lives in a small town in Mississippi. She seems to like it there, and I thought I might go visit. If I like it well enough, I'll find a job and stay there. Otherwise, I'll move on until I find the place to call home."

Griffin's jaw tightened. "You have a home, Delilah. Here. What do you think Dad will say? Or Mom? You'll break her heart."

No, I wouldn't. I'd already had this discussion with her, and while she wasn't ready for me to move on, she understood. Besides, she knew exactly how I felt. My mother loved her life with my dad, but we'd talked enough about her past for me to know she'd felt stifled by her father. She'd gone against him to stay with my dad. Back then, Dad had been a mechanic at a rundown shop on the wrong side of town. Now he owned three garages with a towing service called Camelot. I still rolled my eyes but had to admit it was a little cute since my dad was Lance and my mom was Gwen.

"You can't talk me out of this, Griffin. I'm old enough to go off on my own. I don't need your permission, or anyone else's. In case you've forgotten, I'm an adult."

He folded his arms and leaned back in the booth. "Only children feel the need to tell people they're adults."

I refrained from sticking my tongue out at him and proving his point. I might only be twenty, but at twenty-five, Griffin wasn't exactly a wise old man. Merely a smartass who thought he knew everything and liked to give me orders. I couldn't deny he'd had my back more times than I could count, but I was tired of him trying to run my life. Between him, Ben, and James, I'd never get to experience life to the fullest. If I didn't make mistakes, how would I learn anything?

For that matter, I'd had to take my own virginity with a sex toy because they never let any guy get close enough for me to experience the real thing. If I didn't move away, I'd end up dying alone with a hundred cats.

"When's the last time you went on a date?" I asked.

He shrugged. "Last night. Why?"

I leaned forward, putting my elbows on the table. "Because my last date was over six months ago, and it was over in all of twenty minutes thanks to Ben barging in and ruining everything. Not one single guy in this town has asked me out since, and they aren't likely to either. Between you, Ben, and James, I can't make it through an entire date. You're fucking up my life, Griffin. I love you, all of you, but I need some space. I'm never going to get it here."

I still remembered the one and only time I'd tried to go to the Dixie Reapers compound for a party. It was a year ago, and I'd already turned nineteen. I'd hoped to finally experience sex with another person and not something that required batteries. Ben had caught me at the gate and hauled me home. I'd been so embarrassed and never attempted to get inside there again. I'd heard the stories but didn't think it could be as wild as people said. I remembered some of their kids from school. While it was true, Farrah had been rather rowdy, the others hadn't seemed so bad. They'd all been a bit younger than me, even Farrah.

"I'm not asking permission," I said. "I have some money saved up, a car, and don't need anything else. I'm leaving whether any of you like it or not. It's not like I won't ever come home."

Griffin stood and tossed some money onto the table, even though our food hadn't arrived yet. "I can't stand back and watch you ruin your life, Delilah. If you wanted my blessing, I'm sorry. I can't give it."

"I wish you didn't feel that way," I said. I'd known this wouldn't go well, but I'd hoped he'd at least try to listen and understand. "Mom already knows. My bags are packed and I'm leaving today."

He stormed off and I worried he'd never forgive me. Didn't he realize I had to grow up? I couldn't live here the rest of my life with my brothers running off every guy I tried to date. Too short, too tall, a player, too nerdy. They'd come up with one excuse after another, but it boiled down to them not wanting me to have a boyfriend.

I'd had enough.

My phone jingled with a text from Missy. *You on the road yet?*

I quickly typed a response. *Not yet. Need to eat.*

Hurry the fuck up! I can't wait to tell you more about the job I have.

She'd alluded to a racy job, one my parents and brothers would hate, but she hadn't given a lot of details. Missy had sworn she wasn't a prostitute or call girl, so there was that small blessing. I didn't begrudge anyone earning a living however they needed, or wanted, to but I knew I'd never make it in that sort of profession.

Still… I hoped I wasn't about to go down a path of ruin I'd never recover from. It was one thing to leave home and try to be independent and another to fall so far there was no way back.

My food arrived and I dug in, refusing to let Griffin ruin my appetite. Besides, if I wanted to make it by nightfall to my new home, I'd need all the fuel I could get. I hated stopping on road trips when I was alone. If I didn't need gas or a bathroom, I wasn't about to get off the highway. I'd heard too many horror stories of women raped or abducted from rest stops or other isolated places.

I finished my meal and headed out to my car. What I hadn't told Griffin was that everything was already stored in the trunk of my Camaro. I loved my car and ran my fingers over the bright yellow paint. It was a few years old and looked like Bumblebee in the *Transformers* movie. The car had been a bone of contention between my dad and grandpa, but they'd finally compromised. Grandpa insisted on gifting me a car when I graduated high school, and Dad had refused to let him give me a "foreign piece of shit." I hadn't cared what car I got as long as it didn't fall apart.

Before I left town, I needed to make one stop. I knew my dad and Ben would be at the garage over on

Pearson Avenue. I pulled into the lot and braced myself, not knowing if this would be a mistake or not. Dad would either get mad and tell me good riddance, get pissed and yell that I wasn't going anywhere, or he'd hug me and wish me well. I wasn't counting on option three since I was his only daughter.

Ben waved at me as I walked past and went into Dad's office, and I quietly closed the door. He had his feet kicked up on the desk, the phone to his ear. He gave me the *just a minute* gesture, holding one finger up, so I stood and waited. After he wrapped up his call, he got up and hugged me tight.

"Haven't had you drop by my work in a while," he said.

"Well, I needed to talk to you about something. And I'm kind of hoping if there are witnesses you won't try to kidnap me and toss me into the back of your truck."

He took a step back, frowning. "Why would I do that?"

I sucked in a breath and braced myself. Mom had taken it well, but I had a feeling Dad would be more like Griffin. I'd been his little girl for so long, and he wasn't ready to let go. Even when I'd checked out colleges, he'd insisted I not go far from home. Which was why I hadn't gone at all.

"Because I'm leaving town. I'm moving."

He stared and didn't move or make a sound. My fingers twitched and I shifted my weight.

"I'm twenty, Dad, and I can't live with you and Mom forever. It's time I made my own way in the world. With Griffin, Ben, and James always lurking in the shadows, I never get a chance to do anything fun around here. I can't have a boyfriend or any sort of normal life. So I'm going to move closer to Missy. I'll only be a day's drive away and it's not like I'll never come home." I stopped rambling and realized my dad was far quieter than he'd ever been in my entire life.

"Does your mom know?" he asked.

I gave a quick nod and hoped I hadn't just started a fight between my parents. My dad adored my mom, but they'd had some fights that I'd thought would bring the house down. The longer he went without saying anything, the more nervous I became. I shifted, moving slightly closer to the door in case I needed to run for it.

"Guess I can't keep you home," he said softly. "You better send your address when you get there and call every day. If I don't hear from you, I'm coming to make sure you're okay. Understood?"

My mouth opened and shut a few times before I found my words. "I understand. Thank you, Daddy. I'd thought this would be harder. Griffin didn't react well."

My dad grunted. "Figures you'd tell your mom and brothers before me."

I moved closer, putting my arms around him. I rested my cheek on his chest and hugged him tight. "Maybe I was saving my favorite for last. Although, I only managed to tell Griffin. He took it so badly, I chickened out before I could tell the others."

He sighed and ran his hand down my hair. "Feels like I'm losing my little girl. Love you, Delilah. To the moon and back."

"Love you too, Daddy. I'll always be your little girl, but it's time for me to go live my life. I can't promise I won't make bad decisions, but I'll learn from them. You don't have to worry. You and Mom taught me everything I need to know in order to stand on my own two feet."

He pressed a kiss to my forehead and gave me a nudge. "Go on then. Get on the road and be careful."

I left his office before I was tempted to stay longer. Leaving my dad had been harder than I'd thought it would be. Ben's eyes flashed with anger as I walked out into the bay where he'd been working on a car. Either he'd overheard my conversation with Dad, or Griffin had called him.

"Love you, Ben," I said. "It's not forever. I just need some space."

"When you fall on your ass, don't call me to pick you back up," he muttered then turned his back on me.

It hurt, but I tried to be understanding. After the way Ben and Griffin had reacted, there was no way I was saying bye to James in person. I'd call from somewhere along the way or after I reached my destination.

I got in my car and hit the road, not looking back.

I only hoped I was doing the right thing.

Chapter One

Titan -- Two Months Later

I leaned back in my chair, mesmerized by the wanton little angel filling my computer screen. She'd blown into town a few months ago, and it hadn't been long before Missy brought her around for a job. Even though Hades Abyss would never exploit women, the girls had come to us for protection. Three of the rooms at the back of the clubhouse had been converted for their business.

But this one... Delilah. I'd known she was special the moment I set eyes on her. Which was why the little show she was putting on wasn't viewed by anyone except me. I'd made sure of it. Wizard had orders to give me a direct feed from her webcam every time she was scheduled. She didn't realize all the money came from my wallet and not countless viewers. Even though she didn't earn as much as the others, it didn't seem to bother her.

Her lips parted as she pinched her nipples, her gaze on the camera. "Do you like that? Want more?"

Fuck yes! I waited, knowing what would happen next.

"Twenty dollars and I'll use the vibrating nipple clamps," the little temptress said.

I clicked the button. Wizard had worked his magic so it appeared she had at least five men viewing her show. I was able to bid as each one in order to keep up the ruse. The moment I'd realized what she'd intended to do, I'd put Wizard to work on this setup. No fucking way anyone was going to watch her except me. I'd gut any asshole who dared, which was why the men in the club gave her a wide berth. They were nice enough, not a single one would do more than share a drink with her.

She picked up the toys and clipped first one then the other to her nipples and turned them on. Delilah moaned and tossed her head back. "Feels so good. Another ten and I'll turn up the speed."

Her gaze flicked to her screen and I pressed the button for a bid from another alias. She smiled and made the clamps vibrate harder. Her eyes went dark as her back arched. Jesus but she was fucking beautiful. My dick was hard as granite as I watched her little performance, bidding for each thing she did during her show. What I really wanted was to make her come in person, to feel her wet heat around my dick as I pounded into her sweet little pussy.

She held up a dildo, small compared to me. She licked the tip and my cock jerked. I unfastened my pants for some relief, feeling like the denim was going to strangle my dick. When she sucked the head of the dildo into her mouth, I knew I was a goner. I reached for the lube I kept at my desk just for her shows and slicked my hand before gripping my cock. I stroked as she worked the toy in and out of her mouth, wishing she was kneeling at my feet right now.

"So good," she murmured. "But it would be even better somewhere else... My pussy? Or my ass?"

Fuck! My heart hammered in my chest.

"Twenty for my pussy or fifty for my ass," she said.

I quickly bid the fifty, then just to make sure she took the bait, I upped it another ten from a different alias. She reached for her own bottle of lube and saturated the dildo before working some of the oil into her ass. She licked the suction cup on the bottom and stuck it to the floor, then adjusted herself so I'd have a side view of her fucking herself with the toy.

She was a Goddamn goddess. My own personal porn star.

"Oh, it burns!" She bit her lip, her eyes wide. "I think I need some encouragement."

The website had some preprogrammed options and I pushed the one for the small vibrator. Every last one of her damn shows cost me several hundred dollars when it was all said and done, and some had even cost closer to a grand, but I didn't fucking care. She was worth it. The toy buzzed to life and she rubbed it around her clit before thrusting it into her pussy.

My hand worked my cock faster, harder. As she slowly sank onto the dildo, taking it into her ass, I came, sticky white cum covering my hand and shirt. And my damn dick was still rock hard. I always came multiple times when I watched her, even though I was getting too damn old to be acting like a randy teenager. Hell, I was pushing forty. Most men I knew who were my age, or a little older, needed at least a few hours to go again. Maybe she just inspired me.

I watched as she fucked her ass with the dildo and worked her pussy with the vibrator. When she came, her release coated her thighs and her body trembled. If I'd been able to see her nipples, I knew they'd be hard little pebbles. Perfect for sucking and biting. I upped my bids so she'd keep going. I made her come three more times before her show ended, and I'd come again as well.

I quickly cleaned myself up and shut down my computer before exiting my office. The rooms where the girls held their shows had a small bathroom where they could shower and change after. I didn't lurk in the hall like a creeper, but I did stick to the end of the bar nearest the rooms while I nursed a beer. When Delilah came out, her cheeks rosy and a smile on her lips, I wanted to wrap her in my arms and kiss the hell out of her.

"Have a good show?" I asked with a wink.

Her smile broadened. "Always. I wasn't too loud, was I?"

"If you get a salute from every guy in here, then it just means you're doing your job right. We don't have to watch. Just listening to you is enough to make men want to fuck you."

Her cheeks went crimson and she ducked her head, but not before I saw a pleased little grin on her lips. She was a contradiction. Bold and sassy enough to do a live webcam show of her getting herself off for money, but in person she seemed almost shy at times. It was cute as fuck, just like her. I reached out and ran my fingers through her hair, unable to help myself.

"I like it," I said. When she'd first arrived, her hair had been a medium brown, not too far off from the color of my hair. Since I'd last seen her, she'd dyed it black with purple streaks. It made her look as pale as Snow White, and her vivid blue eyes stood out even more.

She came a little closer, her fingers tightening on the strap of her bag giving an indication she might be nervous. "Thank you. Not just for the compliment, but for giving us a safe place to work. I know the club takes a cut, but it's better than trying to do this at the apartment. I'd be scared someone would find me."

"Not going to let anything hurt you, angel." I stroked my finger down her nose, then leaned back a little so I wouldn't be tempted to do far more. Shit. She had to be half my age. The fact she never tried to get a drink, other than asking for a bottle of water or a soda, made me wonder if she was even twenty-one. I knew she was legal or she wouldn't be able to do the webcam show at all.

Missy had come to us with the idea a year ago and she'd hashed out the details with the club officers. We got twenty percent from each girl to not only offer protection, but Missy also paid Wizard to set up the site and the programming required for it to work. The woman had started her own company and she'd been smart about it. For a fee, Wizard tracked all the people using the site and made sure it remained operational. How she handled payment to the girls working for her was her business and hers alone.

I always felt bad taking any money from Delilah. Hell, I was the only one paying her. When she paid her twenty percent each week, it was like she'd paid *me* to watch her get off. Shit. And now I was getting hard again.

"I also wanted to thank you for not... not making me feel like..." She bit her lip and looked away.

"Like a whore?" I asked.

She gave a jerky nod and glanced at me. "I know what I'm doing isn't exactly conventional. Some guys might consider it prostitution and think they had a right to take what they wanted. I feel safe here. No one ever says anything bad to me. The few who do make remarks are always teasing."

"You know Missy comes here even when she's not doing her show, right?" I asked. I wasn't so sure my brothers were only teasing. Delilah was hot as hell and I knew every damn one of the men in my club would gladly have her on her back, bent over a table, or on her knees. Then I'd have to bust their damn heads. I'd already started to think of her as mine, even though we seldom interacted with one another. They knew how I felt about her, but it didn't mean they didn't want her just the same.

"Yeah, she said she likes to party with the club. She's tried to get me to come with her."

I straightened, towering over her. "Don't come to the parties at the clubhouse. You hear me, Delilah?"

Her eyes went wide, and she paled a little before anger tightened her features. "I'm not a child, Titan. If I want to attend a party, I will. It's why I left home, so I could have a life. I didn't trade one dad for another."

Ouch. "Dad? You think I'm your second daddy?"

She visibly swallowed and tried to take a step back, but I reached out and grabbed hold of her arm, yanking her toward me. I leaned down, and my gaze locked with hers.

"Then maybe I ought to turn you over my knee and spank you."

She gasped and swayed toward me. And in that moment, I knew it was a lost cause. There was no fucking way I'd ever be able to walk away from her. I kissed her. Hard. My tongue thrust between her lips as I took what I wanted, bent her to my will, and had her whimpering for more. Her hands fisted my cut as she clung to me. I wound her long hair around my hand, anchoring her.

I'd always been a demanding man in the bedroom, and it wasn't something I'd change anytime soon. I liked being in control. The way she melted against me told me enough. She might have some spunk, but deep down, she was a submissive little thing. She'd take my orders and love every second of it.

I nipped her jaw, then put my lips by her ear. "You want to come to a party? Want to know what will happen?"

Her breath came out fast and hard, as if she'd just run a marathon.

"You'd be stripped, put on display in front of the entire club. Girls who come to party aren't allowed to tell a brother no. They tell you to drop to your knees and suck their dicks, you'd better damn well do it. They want to ride your ass in front of everyone, you'd have to let them." I tightened my hold on her hair, making her give a little cry of distress. "My sweet little Delilah, you'd be entering the wolf's den, and you wouldn't be the same when you left. Your little show is hot as fuck, but it's safe. You come here to party, any night, and I'll know. You'll leave me no choice but to punish you."

I backed off and released her. She stumbled, grabbing onto the bar for support. Her eyes were dark with need, her lips parted, and fuck if I didn't want to toss her over my shoulder and find the nearest bed.

"You don't come here to party unless you're willing to pay the price. Understood?" I asked.

She nodded, hitched her bag higher on her shoulder, and took off like hellhounds were chasing her. I sat back on the stool and finished my beer before getting another. It hadn't been her fault. She'd not known I'd do anything to be the one fucking her instead of the plastic toys she owned. Although, I'd tipped my hand with the comment about her show. Fucking hell.

I ran a hand down my face. It had taken everything in me to not chase after her -- and keep her. I knew from what Missy had shared they came from the same town as the Dixie Reapers. When I'd first found out where Missy had grown up, I'd worried she was related to a Reaper. She'd assured me that wasn't the case. The moment I'd seen Delilah, I'd hoped like fuck she didn't belong to one either. It would have complicated things, but Missy said Delilah had no ties to the club. Although, she'd hinted at the parties she'd attended there, so I'd invited her to stop by any night. She'd come through the clubhouse doors a night later and nearly every night since.

The thought of Delilah coming to party had me grinding my teeth. If I saw her walk through those doors, she'd be over my shoulder and out of here before she had time to protest. Then I'd spank her ass, tie her down, and show her she didn't need anyone's dick but mine. I didn't know how she'd gotten under my skin so fast, but the moment I'd seen her it was like I'd been hit by lightning. If anyone had ever told me love at first sight existed, I'd have laughed and called them an idiot. Until her.

I didn't know that I was necessarily in love with the woman, but I was definitely in lust. And a bit obsessed. I found myself eagerly anticipating the days she'd be here filming her webcam show. Yeah, I always got off while I watched her, but it was more than that. The short interactions we had before or after were just as important to me. I liked hearing what she had to say, being close enough to smell her sweet scent.

"You ever going to make a move?" my VP, Boomer, asked.

"Thought I just did."

He snorted. "No, but you did give her something to think about. Not sure why you let her leave. You've been wanting that one in your bed for months. Why not just get her out of your system?"

I didn't think it would be so simple. No, now that I'd had even the slightest taste, I found I wanted her even more. I didn't think fucking her would make me lose interest. If anything, I'd probably want to keep her. Since she showed up, I'd let the club whores suck me off a few times that first week, but every damn time I'd closed my eyes and pictured Delilah on her knees. I always felt like shit afterward and hadn't been tempted to let them anywhere near me in over a month.

My brothers had noticed, but only Boomer had the balls to say anything. He'd known right off I'd let Delilah get under my skin, and he took great pleasure in giving me shit about it. For one, she was young enough to be my daughter. It's part of why I hadn't made a move. Until now. I could only imagine what Phoebe would think of me dating someone her age or younger. I'd only just discovered I even had a daughter. Last thing I wanted to do was run her off.

I saw Kraken across the room. He adored my daughter and was a great dad to their kids. Hell, I still wasn't used to being called Grandpa, but I had to admit my granddaughter had me wrapped around her finger. Much like my daughter. The fact some bitch had gotten knocked up way back when, then dropped my kid with a sadistic preacher pissed me the fuck off. If the woman wasn't already dead and buried, I'd have put her in a grave myself. I'd tried tracking her down, only to find out she'd died a few years after abandoning our daughter.

I made my way over to Kraken and claimed the seat next to him, setting my beer on the table. He and my daughter had been together a little over year now, and Phoebe had blossomed during her time here. When I thought of all she'd suffered, I wanted to kill everyone responsible. Kraken had beaten me to it.

"The kids asked when you're going to come see them," Kraken said.

I arched an eyebrow. "Really? Ember I can believe, but you're telling me six-month-old Banner asked about me?"

It still hurt to think about the baby they'd lost. Banner had been a twin, but the cord had been wrapped around his brother's neck and the baby had been stillborn. It had devastated Phoebe and Kraken, but I knew they were trying to move forward best they could and stay upbeat for the kids.

Kraken grinned. "Yep."

I snorted and flipped him off. The kid was smart, but not that damn smart. Ember on the other hand was a borderline genius from what I could tell, and I wasn't just bragging. The kid scared me sometimes with how intelligent she was for only being two.

"Let me ask you something." I picked at the label on my beer bottle. "You think Phoebe would be upset if I started seeing someone?"

"Would it be a certain little sex goddess you just kissed and let run away?" he asked.

"Maybe." I rotated the bottle, twisting it around and around. "She's probably about Phoebe's age. I don't want to weird out my daughter, but there's something about Delilah. I can't stop thinking about her."

"You really think my woman would ever begrudge you happiness? Shit, Titan. We're damn near the same age and she doesn't have a problem with me being older than her. You really think she'll care if you date a younger woman?"

When he put it that way…

"Guess I'll wait and see what happens. She mentioned possibly coming to a party here. I let her know she'd be punished if she did. No fucking way I'm letting her partake in the shit that goes down in the clubhouse at night. Anyone so much as touches her and I'll gut the fucker. Brother or not."

Kraken nodded. "I think we all got that memo. Everyone knows you pay to watch her webcam thing and won't let it stream live. They also know she isn't aware of that little fact."

Part of me wanted her to give the club a wide berth when she wasn't filming. The other part... Well, the bastard inside me wanted her to come here, give me a reason to spank her ass, and do so much more. There's probably a seat waiting for me on the right-hand side of Lucifer when I arrive in hell, but for now, I'd take my pleasure where I can... and little Delilah had me tied up in knots. If I got off just watching her, multiple times, then what would it be like to fuck her?

Kraken cleared his throat. "Look, Pres. No one here is going to touch your girl. But out there is another matter. She doesn't live at the compound. Plenty of places for her to find a guy. A woman who gets herself off to make money, and doesn't care who's watching, probably isn't sitting home on a Friday night. Just saying... maybe it's time to let her know you want her."

I thought I'd already done that. Only time would tell. We had a party later tonight, and I knew Missy would be here. I'd watch and see if Delilah showed up with her. If she did, then I'd let her know the only damn bed she would be in was mine.

Chapter Two

Delilah

Shock. Anger. Confusion. Need. I'd felt them all since Titan had kissed me. I didn't know why he'd done it. I wasn't anything special. Compared to Missy, I was rather plain. I knew several of the women who frequented the Hades Abyss MC parties, and each was stunning in their own way. They stood out. Other than my new hair color, there wasn't a single remarkable thing about me.

So why had he done it? To put me in my place? To scare me? Or was it something more? Maybe a promise... There was only one way I'd ever find out. He'd said I'd be punished if I came to a party. The mere thought of the President of Hades Abyss being the one to dole out that punishment had my nipples tightening and my panties getting damp. From what Missy had said, he hadn't touched a woman in over a month. No one knew why, but surely he wasn't seeing anyone on a regular basis if he'd kissed me earlier.

I smoothed my hand over my messy hair. I should have straightened it, but I'd been too nervous about tonight. Instead, it hung in a riot of curls, waves, and no little amount of frizz, making me look like a wild woman. Or an escaped lunatic. I felt a little crazy at the moment.

Since leaving home, I'd become a different person. It wasn't just my hair that I'd changed. I had a new wardrobe, thanks to the money I'd been making at my job. I'd also become bolder, or so I'd thought. The moment Titan had towered over me, leaned into my space, I'd reverted back to the insecure girl who'd never been kissed. If I hadn't taken my own virginity with a sex toy, I'd still be a virgin.

"Missy, are you sure about this?" I asked.

"Honey, if Titan threatened you, then it means he's hoping you'll show up."

I stared at her, not quite comprehending how she'd come to that conclusion. He'd said *not* to come to a party. Then again, Missy knew far more about men than I ever would. Thanks to my brothers, I'd never had a steady boyfriend. I'd thought coming here would change things for me, but I hadn't felt comfortable the few times I'd been asked out. The way they'd looked at me had made my skin crawl. It was one thing to be on the webcam, naked and having fun, because I was paid to do it and enjoyed myself. Yeah, I knew people were watching, but I didn't see them. The guys who asked me out always made me feel like they were trying to see through my clothes, and only wanted to get laid.

I wanted sex. With a person. It wasn't that I was saving myself for anyone special. Maybe at one point I had been, but not anymore. It also didn't mean I planned to drop my panties for the first guy to pay me some attention. I wasn't desperate. Not exactly.

Before I could change my mind, Missy grabbed my arm and started dragging me from the apartment we shared. Rissa, another webcam girl, followed in our wake. Both of them looked far sexier than me. I was certain if they bent over the entire world would see their panties, assuming they were wearing any. Considering the lack of lines, I was betting on either a thong or nothing at all. It made me feel overdressed. I tugged at the hem of my skirt, which hit me mid-thigh and flared out a bit. The dress I'd put on was cute, but standing next to Missy and Rissa, I looked like I was going out on a date and not to a party at the clubhouse. Did all the women dress like that?

"I don't think this is a good idea," I said. "I'm not dressed right."

Missy snorted. "Please. Do you think the Pres is going to care what you're wearing? The simple fact you're there will be enough. Trust me, Delilah. The man wants you."

I let her shove me into the backseat of her car and I accepted my fate. If things didn't go according to plan, I could always try to call an Uber. Assuming there *was* an Uber service in this tiny little town. I knew we couldn't get food delivery, which sucked on days I didn't feel like getting out of the apartment.

Missy and Rissa chatted on the way there, but my stomach was twisting into knots. I was both scared and excited about seeing Titan again. I'd noticed him months ago when I'd arrived in town and Missy had taken me to the clubhouse to show me the rooms used for the webcam site. Even though I knew he was older than me, probably by quite a bit, there had been something about the man that lured me in. I'd had a hard time looking away.

His words from earlier came back to haunt me. *Your little show is hot as fuck...* Did that mean he watched it? My cheeks burned at the thought of such a sexy man paying to see me. I used an alias so my online customers wouldn't be able to find me, but Titan knew exactly where I was the entire time. Had he been watching from the beginning?

"We're here," Missy said as the car came to a stop.

I took a breath and braced myself. After Titan's warning earlier about what to expect, and talking to Missy a bit more, I was scared as hell about going in there. If he wasn't there, or had only been trying to run me off, and the men inside actually expected me to… to…

"I don't think I can," I said, shrinking back into the seat.

"Of course you can," Rissa said. "If Titan isn't here, then just have a good time with someone else. It's just sex, Delilah."

Just. Sex. Maybe for her, but since I'd never had sex with anyone, it was far more to me. I took a breath and got out of the car. The girls ran ahead of me, rushing up the steps and into the clubhouse, obviously eager for whatever awaited them inside. I, on the other hand, dragged my feet and felt like I was going to my execution. As I pushed through the doors, my eyes went wide and my mouth dropped open.

Women were scattered around the room in various states of undress. Several were either giving blowjobs or getting fucked over tables and against walls. What the hell had I agreed to? It looked more like an orgy than a party. Missy hadn't been inside more than two minutes and already her top was off and her breasts were bare.

I felt my cheeks warm as I scanned the room. The moment my gaze landed on Titan, I froze. He looked me over from head to toe, like a predator observing his prey. When he stood and made his way over to me, it felt like my heart would beat out of my chest. What the hell had I gotten myself into? I glanced around the room again and wondered if I could run right back outside and pretend I'd never been here.

Titan stopped in front of me and I forced myself to look up. His jaw was tight, and a hint of anger flickered in his eyes.

"I warned you, Delilah. What did I say would happen if you came here to party?" he asked.

"I'd be punished," I said. "I didn't think you meant it."

He waved a hand at the room. "Is this what you want? Every patched brother in here fucking your brains out? Possibly even more than one of them at a time?"

I gasped and took a step back, but he reached out, grabbing my arm to keep me still. He moved in closer, the heat of his body pressing against me. My breath caught as I tried not to run.

He tipped my chin up. "Why are you here?"

"Not for..." I waved my hand at everyone. "This isn't a party. Parties have music, drinks, dancing."

"We have all that. And more."

"It's the more part I wasn't prepared for. I thought you were only trying to scare me earlier. I didn't know you meant every word." My cheeks burned even hotter. "Just because I'm on the webcam site doesn't mean I'm a whore."

He backed me up and out onto the porch of the clubhouse. Once the chaos inside was shut away again, I breathed a little easier.

"Those women are considered club whores, but they're here of their own free will. They like what they do. It's fun. For them and for us."

"Us?" I asked.

He smirked. "Did you think I was a monk?"

"Well, no, but Missy said..." I clamped my lips shut.

"She said what?" he asked, his voice a near growl.

"That you hadn't been with anyone lately."

He studied me. Quiet. Intense. His gaze pinned me in place, and I couldn't have run if I wanted to.

"Do you know why?" he asked.

I shook my head and hoped like hell he wasn't about to tell me he had a girlfriend, or worse, a wife. Of course, if he did and he'd planned to partake of the activities inside it made him a cheater. I really hated cheaters.

"Because two months ago the sexiest, sweetest little thing walked into my clubhouse and I haven't been able to stop thinking about her." He smiled a little. "That would be you, in case you didn't figure it out. I want you, Delilah. The question is whether or not you want me. I've never taken what wasn't offered."

He stroked my hair and a shiver raked my spine.

"Will you offer yourself to me?" he asked.

It felt like there was a lump in my throat that wouldn't go down. I mutely nodded, hoping I hadn't made a huge mistake. Titan lifted me into his arms and carried me down to his bike. He settled me on the seat and showed me where to put my feet before he got on. Reaching back, he grabbed my wrists and pulled my hands around his waist.

"Hold on, little girl. Don't want you falling off."

I snorted. "I'm not little."

I really wasn't. I might be short compared to his monstrous height, but I was too curvy, too chunky to be considered little. My mom had always told me men would love my curves. I wasn't stupid. Even I knew the plus-size models had nipped-in waists. They might not be size two, but they didn't have what I called my Buddha belly either. At least, not the ones I'd seen modeling clothes for my favorite shops. Those women were sexy. I was just… fat. It didn't stop me from eating whatever I wanted when I wanted, but I also wouldn't lie to myself. I knew I needed to watch my weight a little, get into better shape.

The fact a man like Titan wanted me was... a little unreal. I felt like pinching myself to see if I'd drifted to sleep and had dreamed tonight.

Titan backed the bike from the space and then eased down the road that wound through the compound. It seemed his place wasn't far because we'd barely gone anywhere before he pulled into a driveway and under a carport. My heart slammed against my ribs as I realized this was really happening. I would finally know what it felt like to have sex with a guy.

What if I was bad at it?

I trembled as I got off the bike and followed meekly in his wake. He led me into his house. I heard the door shut and looked up at him. Titan pinned me to the door, his body pressing against mine.

"Last chance to change your mind," he said. "If you're going to bolt, do it now."

I shook my head. I wanted this. Wanted him. If I embarrassed myself, I'd have to find a new job and avoid the Hades Abyss compound at all costs. I'd never be able to look him in the eye if I screwed up tonight. Good thing I'd been putting money away in case of an emergency. Not living up to Titan's expectations in the bedroom would certainly qualify.

He lowered his head, his lips pressing to mine. I parted them and he took advantage, thrusting his tongue into my mouth. My knees went weak as he devoured me, bending me to his will. There was no other way to think of it, what little thinking I could do. When he backed up, I found myself leaning toward him, not wanting him to stop.

Titan smirked and took my hand, leading me away from the front entry. We walked up a flight of stairs and past several doorways. I was curious about his home. Not enough to ask for a tour right that very moment. No, right now, I wanted more of his kisses, and... other things. He pushed open a door and I gawked at the room.

The walls were a slate gray, the carpet under my feet felt plush and I sank with every step. The bed had a charcoal comforter with black pinstripes. Even from several feet away I could tell the material was heavy and costly. Despite what I earned off the webcam site, I'd never have a place like this one. I wondered if the house was a perk for being President of the club.

"You're still dressed," he said.

I turned and my eyes went wide as I studied his body. He'd already stripped off his cut and shirt, as well as his boots, socks, and jeans. All that remained were a pair of boxer briefs. They molded to his body, and the extremely hard ridge of his cock. My breath caught. I'd never had anything so large inside me and I was a little worried he wouldn't fit.

"Getting shy on me now?" he asked. "Men stare at you every week. Different in person?"

"I, um..." I licked my lips. "I haven't..."

How exactly did I tell him he would be my first? Even if I didn't have a hymen anymore, I was technically a virgin. I'd never sucked a real cock or had one inside me. I'd never truly been kissed. Most of the guys I'd tried dating were run off before they felt comfortable kissing me. My brothers made sure of it.

He prowled closer, reaching for me. Gently tugging on a lock of my hair, he studied me. I wondered what he saw when he looked at me. I'd noticed the women at the clubhouse. They were all fit, or no larger than my thigh. Would he be disappointed? He'd made the comment about this being different in person, but what if he didn't like my rounded belly when it wasn't on his phone or computer screen?

I'd never been sensitive about my weight, not since middle school. I knew I wasn't going to walk a runway, and I was fine with that. It wasn't something I ever aspired to. But having a man look at me like I was the most delicious thing he'd ever seen? That was definitely on my bucket list, and I'd found that men who looked like Titan didn't pay much attention to curvier girls.

"Baby, look at me," he said, his voice deep yet gentle.

My gaze jerked from his cock to his face.

"You look both excited and scared. What's wrong?" he asked.

I bit my lip, deciding he needed to know. It wasn't like he'd hurt me. I wouldn't bleed or anything.

"I haven't done this before," I admitted.

"If you're thinking this is a one-night stand, I hadn't planned for that to be the case. I have a feeling just once won't be anywhere near enough."

"It's not what I meant."

He slid his hand around the back of my neck, drawing me closer. The tenderness in his eyes was almost enough to make me run. No one had ever looked at me like that. The fact it was the big, bad President of Hades Abyss made my stomach twist.

"Talk to me, Delilah. If you've changed your mind, just say so."

"I haven't. But you may if I tell you what I meant." He just stared me down. "I haven't done this before. As in sex. With someone other than me."

His eyebrows rose. "You've only gotten yourself off, but you've never been with a person? Is that what you're saying?"

I nodded, my cheeks burning.

"Well, fuck me," he muttered. "I knew you were special. Didn't realize until now you were a Goddamn unicorn. A virgin who has a webcam show. And before you ask, yes, I watch your show. Every damn time. Hottest fucking thing I've ever seen."

"You're not disappointed?"

He gave a bark of laughter. "Disappointed? Not fucking likely. You sure you want me to be your first?"

"Yes. More than anything."

He gathered me closer, holding me tight against his body. "And if I want to be your last?"

I stared up at him, unsure what to say. He couldn't be serious, could he?

"You on birth control?" he asked.

"Yes." I'd only started it about two weeks ago, but I did take it regularly. I'd hoped I'd have the chance to have sex with someone before too long. Looked like my wish was coming true.

"I'm clean, baby. Got tested after the last time I was with a woman. You trust me enough to take you bare?"

My heart crashed against my ribs. "Yes," I said softly.

I shouldn't. I really shouldn't. Even though I'd met him two months ago, I didn't know much about him. What if he was lying? Although, Missy had said he hadn't been with anyone lately. Didn't mean he hadn't been when she wasn't around. Still, if he said he was clean and hadn't been with anyone, then I'd trust him.

He gripped the hem of my dress and lifted the material over my head. He groaned as he stared at my lace-covered breasts. I'd worn my best bra. Black lace that left little to the imagination, and the panties matched. They were the cheeky kind and had a tendency to ride up my butt, which I hated, but I felt pretty in them. Desirable.

"Damn, baby." He slid his hand down the slope of one breast. "So soft. Perfect."

"Not perfect."

He growled softly and before I realized what was happening, he'd sat and pulled me over his lap, and his hand cracked against my ass. I squeaked as he smacked both cheeks until they felt like they were on fire.

"Did you sass me?" he asked, his hand coming down again and again.

"I-I'm sorry, Titan."

Smack. Smack. Smack.

An enraged barking started at the door, and what sounded like a hellhound trying to claw its way into the room. I tensed and squirmed, trying to get free. What the hell was in the hallway?

"Sorry? You're fucking sorry? Don't disrespect me by saying shit about this fucking sexy body. You've had me hard as fuck since the first moment I saw you. Do you think I like ugly women?"

Smack. Smack. Smack.

What had to be a dog was going nuts outside the door. Did it not bother Titan even a little? He acted as if he hadn't noticed.

"No! I don't, I just…" *Smack. Smack.* "Titan! Stop, please. I'm sorry."

He rubbed both cheeks. When he dipped his hand between my legs, his fingers brushing over my pussy, I moaned and closed my eyes. Even though my ass hurt, it had also been kind of a turn-on. I had no doubt my panties were damp.

"How attached are you to this scrap of lace?" he asked, tugging at the waistband.

"Very. I'm very attached."

He worked the panties over my ass and hips, then down my thighs until he'd pulled them all the way off. He stroked the bare lips of my pussy and I lifted my ass, trying to spread my legs farther. I'd never wanted someone so much in my life! The second he touched my clit I might detonate.

He thrust two fingers inside me, hard and fast. I cried out, my back arching. He worked my pussy with long strokes that had me seeing stars. The wet sounds were enough to tell me I was soaking his hand. God, he felt so good! Far better than anything I had with batteries. Using his other hand, he popped the clasp on my bra.

He removed his fingers from my pussy, right before I could come. I wanted to protest, but Titan flipped me over, twisting and laying me down on the bed. He dragged my bra straps down my arms and tossed the garment aside. The cool air caressed my nipples, making them harden into tight little points.

The way he looked at me, as if he were starving and I was a five-star meal, made me want him even more. The dog was forgotten, as was the pain radiating in my ass cheeks. My brothers had run off any guys before we'd ever had a chance to get this far. Having a man like Titan want me as much as he did was a heady experience.

He stripped out of his underwear and braced his weight as he settled over me. I spread my thighs wider. The heat of his cock, trapped between our bodies, made me want to squirm and beg him to fuck me. I felt like a wanton hussy. Or maybe I'd been reading too many historical romances lately.

"Ready, baby?" he asked.
"I need you, Titan."
"Justin. Call me Justin," he said.

Chapter Three

Titan

I hadn't asked anyone to use my real name in so long, but it felt right with Delilah. When she whispered *Justin*, something settled in my chest, a warmth I hadn't felt before. The moment I'd seen her, I'd known she was special. It just hadn't occurred to me until right now exactly how special.

I blocked out the sound of Barney trying to dig his way under the bedroom door and focused on the angel lying under me. I'd never met anyone her equal. Sexy. Sweet. And mine!

I eased into her, sinking into her silken heat. Fuck but she felt incredible!

I tried to concentrate on her face, hoping I wasn't hurting her. I'd seen the toys she used, and they were small compared to me. It wasn't like I had a twelve-inch monster in my pants, but as small as she was nine inches might be too big.

"You okay, baby?" I asked, fighting to keep control.

"Don't hold back," she said. "I can handle it, Justin. I want to experience everything."

I thrust into her harder. She placed her hands on my shoulders. As I switched my angle, her nails bit into me and her eyes darkened. I should have taken more time with her, but she had me wound so tight I couldn't think straight. I took her. Claimed her. Did my best to ruin her for any other man.

When her pussy squeezed my cock and she cried out as she came, I let go, allowing myself to follow. My balls drew up and on the next stroke I was filling her with my cum. Christ but she was perfect! I twitched inside her, my dick still semi-hard and I knew I could easily go again. Delilah brought out the beast in me.

She reached up and placed her hand on my cheek. "That was wonderful. I can't believe I've missed out on this for so long."

I smiled and leaned down to press my lips to hers. "Darlin', it's not like you've never come before."

"Not the same." She shook her head. "Being with you, coming with your cock inside me, was incredible. Far better than any toy."

I nipped her lip and rolled my hips. My dick was already getting rock hard again. I kissed the hell out of her before flipping to my back, taking her with me. She straddled me, looking startled at the sudden change of position.

"Ride me, beautiful." I reached up to cup her breasts. "I want to see these bounce as you take what you want."

She ran her fingers down my chest to my abs, then braced herself as she lifted until my cock was nearly out of her. Delilah slammed back down, taking every inch, and my eyes almost rolled back into my head. Fuck! She was going to kill me, but it would be a hell of a way to go.

"So fucking gorgeous," I said. I kneaded her breasts, loving how they overflowed my hands. How she'd thought she wasn't sexy was beyond me. "Come for me, baby."

I flicked her nipples with my thumbs as she rode me harder. Giving one of the rigid peaks a pinch sent her over the edge. She screamed out my name, her movements becoming jerky and uncoordinated. I gripped her hips, lifting her a little, then thrust up into her. On the third stroke, I came.

"Jesus, woman. You're going to kill me." She collapsed onto my chest and I ran my fingers through her hair. "I'm too damn old to fuck you twice in a row."

She giggled and lifted her head to look me in the eye. "You're not old, Justin. You're seasoned to perfection."

I swatted her ass. "What am I? A steak?"

She sighed and cuddled closer. "No. You're amazing, that's what you are."

Her words touched me. No one had said that to me before, especially a woman. Oh, there were plenty who wanted my dick or the honor of being the Pres's old lady, but Delilah was something else. She was the perfect mix of naughty and sweet. I'd never wanted to cuddle after sex, but I wasn't ready to let her go. I ran my hand down her back and tangled my other one in her hair. I wanted her to stay.

Shit. I was in trouble. She was the only woman I'd brought to my house, and now I didn't want her to go home. I'd given Kraken shit over Phoebe, before I'd known she was my daughter, and now I was doing the same fucking thing. I wanted to make Delilah mine. Sure, we'd technically known one another for two months, but we'd never had a date. Never shared a kiss until today.

Would I chase her off if I asked her to stay? No, I wouldn't *ask*. Asking was for pussies.

"Was I imagining things or do you have a dog? Because it's either that or Satan unleashed hellhounds and they were trying to break in," she said.

I couldn't help but laugh. "Barney isn't a hellhound, but he *is* determined. I'll introduce you later. Promise he won't eat you."

I reached over and switched off the lamp.

"What are you doing?" she asked, her voice soft and low.

"We're going to get under the covers and get some sleep. When you're rested, I'm going to fuck you again."

She sighed and rubbed her cheek against me. "I should tell you no and go home."

"Should but you won't."

"Cocky," she murmured.

"No. Not cocky. I know what I want. Which is you. Now that I have you in my house, in my bed, you're not leaving until I say you can."

She lifted her head and stared at me. "That's a rather caveman thing to say."

I grinned. "You knew that about me before tonight, darlin'."

She gave an indelicate snort and laid her cheek back on my chest. It seemed she wasn't going to argue or fight me on this, which was good. She'd have lost. If it meant I had to spank her ass again, I would. If I had to tie her to the bed, so be it. Actually… I rather liked that idea. My cock started to get hard inside her again.

Delilah moaned. "Not yet. I need time to recover."

"Baby, you have a webcam show where you get yourself off for an hour. I seriously doubt me fucking you twice made you sore."

"You're bigger than my toys, Justin. Take the compliment and shut up."

I fought not to laugh and swatted her ass again. "Stop sassing me."

"Never," she said in a near whisper. The next moment, her breathing evened out and I knew she'd fallen asleep. It took a bit of maneuvering, the bedding twisted underneath us, but I managed to pull the sheet over us. For the first time in my life, I didn't want to let a woman go. Didn't matter if my arms went to sleep, my legs, or even my dick. I wasn't moving her if I didn't have to.

When we'd come into the bedroom, I'd set my phone on the bedside table out of habit. Now the damn thing was going off and I hoped it didn't wake up Delilah. I reached over and turned it so I could read the screen. *Wizard*.

"What the fuck do you want?" I asked, putting the phone to my ear. "I'm busy, asshole."

"Yeah, I got that. Everyone said you took one look at Delilah and ran off with her. But, Pres, we've got a problem."

Shit. I didn't want, nor need, to hear that right now. "What is it?"

"New webcam girl."

I looked down at Delilah. "She's in my arms. What of her?"

"Not that one. The one who showed up two weeks ago. Shella isn't a name I hear all that often. Struck me as familiar," Wizard said. "Then I remembered. Grizzly had a girl by that name who ran off. Hasn't been back to Devil's Fury in years. It's her, Pres. His kid is doing a webcam show in our fucking clubhouse. If the Devil's Fury finds out, they're going to want a pound of flesh."

Fuck my life. "She's done. I don't want her stepping foot inside the clubhouse again. You hear me? Whatever it takes, you get that girl home where she belongs."

Had she lost her damn mind? If Grizzly found out what she'd been doing, or that we'd allowed it, we'd all be fucking dead. He might not be the President of the Devil's Fury anymore, but I didn't want on his bad side either. And Badger... shit. Shella was his sister-in-law. I could only imagine what the new Devil's Fury Pres would have to say about it.

I set the phone down and held Delilah closer to me. Just having her in my arms made everything seem better. Didn't matter if hell was about to rain down on me or not. She gave me a sense of peace I hadn't felt in a long time, not even after discovering I had a daughter and granddaughter. I loved Phoebe and Ember, and my new grandson, Banner, but they didn't live with me. Kraken had claimed my daughter before I'd even known she was mine.

At nearly forty, I was ready to settle down. The club whores had lost their appeal. Hell, Delilah was the only one who'd had me ready for round two so fast in years. Even now, I could fuck her again. I wasn't a big enough asshole to wake her, though. I enjoyed the weight of her on my chest as she breathed deep and even. It made me wonder how she'd been sleeping since she moved here. Missy had said she was a friend from back home, but that's about all I knew of Delilah.

She stirred against me, and I ran my hand down her back, loving the feel of her soft skin. She stretched and slowly opened her eyes, giving me a shy smile.

"Did I sleep long?" she asked.

"Maybe a half hour."

"Felt like longer." She looked toward the window before sighing. "Guess I better go home."

Home? I tightened my hold on her. "Or you could stay right here."

"I didn't think men like you wanted a woman hanging around too long. Don't you usually kick them out when you're done?" she asked.

"Told you this was different. You're not a one-night stand, Delilah."

"You don't know anything about me, Titan."

I smacked her ass and she yelped. "What's my name?"

"Justin." She smiled a little. "I don't want to overstay my welcome and end up being labeled as one of those clingy women you can't get rid of."

Fat chance of that happening. I wanted her here. "You could tell me about yourself. If you want, I can get us some drinks. We can sit in the living room."

She rested her chin on my chest as she stared at me. I couldn't decipher the look in her eyes, but it was clear I'd surprised her. Did she think I was such an asshole I'd toss her out? Lie just to get in her pants? Or had no one ever wanted more than that from her? The fact she'd never been with a man baffled the shit out of me. A woman as sexy as she was should have had guys beating down her door.

I rolled us so she lay under me, then kissed her soft and slow. She gave a little sigh as I pulled away, a dreamy look in her eyes. I ran my fingers down her cheek before pressing my lips to hers again.

"Come on, baby. You can put on one of my shirts and we'll go get a drink so we can get to know one another better."

I got up, then held out my hand, helping her off the bed. She picked up the shirt I'd been wearing earlier and pulled it over her head. I grabbed my boxer briefs from the floor and put them on, not bothering with anything else. I couldn't remember if I'd locked the front door and didn't want to chance my daughter coming in and catching me naked. She'd done that once a few months ago and we'd both gotten the shock of a lifetime. Needless to say, I always stayed dressed if I wasn't in my bedroom, or at least made sure my cock wasn't hanging out.

Once we were covered enough we wouldn't scandalize Phoebe, or scar her for life, I led her to the kitchen. Barney sniffed at Delilah a few times, licked her ankles, then danced around my feet. I had no doubt he needed to pee. Or bark at the moon. Or the air. Fuck knew he just liked hearing the sound of his voice. I let him out back before opening the fridge.

I had no idea what she'd want. I could make coffee, or I had a jug of sweet tea. I could drink coffee any time of day or night, but I knew most people preferred it in the mornings. There wasn't much else to drink in the fridge other than beer. She didn't strike me as the beer-drinking type.

"Sweet tea, coffee, or tap water?" I asked.

"Tea is fine," she said.

I pulled the gallon jug from the fridge and poured two glasses. Barney scratched at the back door and I let him in. He cocked his head at me. Tongue lolling, he scrabbled over to Delilah, his nails clicking on the floor. She had a soft smile on her face as she reached down to him. Barney licked her fingers and she giggled.

"And that's Barney," I said. "Found him a few months ago, wandering the streets. Or rather, he found *me* on a rainy night. I was heading back to my bike from the liquor store and heard this noise behind me. He followed me all the way to the Harley, then gave me this look that clearly said he expected to go with me. Wasn't easy, but I let him ride with me. Took him to the vet and they said he wasn't microchipped. Looked like he'd been on his own for a while. Skinny. Covered in fleas. He was in rough shape."

"He's beautiful," she said, rubbing Barney's ears. "And sweet!"

Yeah, he was a good dog. Maybe not the sort most people pictured the president of an MC having, but I liked having him around. Not to mention he was smart as hell. He also sounded like a one-hundred-pound German Shepherd when he barked which made him a decent guard dog, as long as no one got a good look at him. Barney didn't exactly inspire fear when you saw him.

I picked up our drinks and motioned for her to follow me to the living room. I eased down onto the couch and she sat next to me, but with a foot of space between us. After I put down the glasses, I reached over and tugged her closer. Barney leapt onto the couch and leaned against her other side.

"So, who is Delilah...? What's your last name, sweetheart?"

"Gilbert," she said. "I'm Delilah Gilbert."

Barney stretched across her lap and she absently rubbed his ears again. He gave a doggy grin and winked at me. If I didn't know better, I'd say he was trying to convince her to stay.

"And, Miss Gilbert, what else should I know about you?" I asked, wrapping my arm around her shoulders and hugging her to me. "Besides the fact you obviously like dogs. Come from a big family? Only child?"

I couldn't imagine any parent being okay with the job she had. It was a good thing I'd made sure no one saw her but me. Even though I didn't know a damn thing about her family, I had no doubt her dad would be pissed if he knew what his little girl was doing for a living. I wasn't too thrilled about it either. She might not be mine -- yet -- but when she was, I'd end her webcam days once and for all. Didn't matter if no other men were lusting after her as she got off.

"Who doesn't like dogs?" she asked. "Especially this one. He's adorable!"

"And he knows it," I said.

"I have three older brothers," she said. "And my parents are still together. My dad used to own a garage and one tow truck. Now he has several locations and more trucks. After he married my mom, he changed the name to Camelot Towing."

"Camelot?" I asked.

Her cheeks turned pink. "My dad's name is Lance and my mom is Gwen. You know, like Lancelot and Guinevere."

Cute. Unexpected for a mechanic to come up with something like that so I was betting on the mom. Then again, just because the guy fixed cars didn't mean he didn't enjoy reading. Maybe he was a King Arthur fan. It was the three older brothers part that made my nape prickle.

"Any chance your family is stopping in for a visit?" I asked.

"No. They were mad I left home. Except Mom. She understood. But my brothers weren't speaking to me when I drove off, and still haven't. I talk to my dad at least every few days. He insisted, so he'd know I was alive and not dead in a ditch."

I made a mental note to have Wizard check into Lance and Gwen Gilbert, as well as Delilah's brothers. I didn't like unknowns and if they decided to show up in town, I wanted to be prepared. Being quite a bit older than her, it was likely her parents and brothers would object to us being together, especially since I was the President of the Mississippi chapter of the Hades Abyss MC. I'd never given a fuck before, and I honestly didn't now, except I wanted her to feel comfortable. Safe. I didn't want Delilah to feel torn between me and her family. Assuming I could convince her to see me again.

"I thought I didn't have any family left. Kraken, my Sergeant-at-Arms, brought a woman home. Decided to keep her, and her little girl. Found out later Phoebe is my daughter. So I'm a grandpa even though I'm not even forty."

She twisted so she could look at me. "Wait, you have a daughter who's old enough to have a kid? How old is she?"

A warning was flashing in my brain to proceed with caution. "Old enough. And yes, I have a daughter. She already had Ember when she came here, but now she and Kraken have a son. Banner. There was another baby, Banner's twin, but he was stillborn."

Her gaze skimmed over me. I knew what she'd see. Lots of ink. I kept in shape so I still had my six-pack even though it was getting harder to maintain than it had been a decade ago. I knew I didn't look like I should be a grandfather. Hell, Kraken was only two years younger than me.

"Phoebe was the product of a one-night stand shortly after I'd patched into the Hades Abyss," I said. "I never knew she existed. If I had, I'd have wanted her. Didn't matter I was still pretty much a kid myself back then. No fucking way would I ever let my daughter grow up without a dad."

"And your daughter isn't going to freak out that you're sleeping with someone around her age?" she asked.

Might be a little weird for her stepmom to be her age, or younger, but we'd make it work. Shit. I was already thinking of keeping Delilah. Knowing I'd been her first was fucking with my head. I'd wanted her before, but now I didn't want to let her go. I didn't think she'd take it well if I claimed her without giving her any say in the matter.

The fact I was going to give her the option of staying or going told me enough. Delilah was unlike anyone I'd met before. Even though she was a webcam girl like Missy, she wasn't ready to strip naked in front of people in person. The look on her face when she'd walked into the clubhouse had been one of horror. I'd warned her what happened.

"Not just sleeping with you, Delilah. You're mine." Well, fuck. I hadn't meant to say that. *Way to take it slow, asshole.* "Exclusive. That's what we are."

Better. Maybe. The way her lips turned down said otherwise.

"Exclusive, or I'm yours because I get the feeling those mean two different things," she said.

"Both. You're mine, which means we're exclusive. I won't fuck other women and you won't fuck other men."

She tipped her head to the side and studied me. It reminded me of the same look Barney gave me when he was deciding if he agreed with me. "Are you asking me or telling me?"

I cracked my neck and tried to hold back the words I wanted to say. Any other woman, I'd lay down the law. But then if Delilah were anyone else, I wouldn't want her this damn bad. She was unique. A combination of sexy and sweet that I couldn't get enough of.

She smiled a little. "So, you're telling me. Got it."

"Something wrong with that?"

"I'm used to men telling me what to do and expecting me to obey. My dad and brothers might not be bikers, but they're definitely the alpha male type. I can't say I'm thrilled to have someone giving me orders, but I like you, Justin. I want to see where this goes."

I lifted her so that she straddled my lap. The fact she didn't fight me said enough. I ran my hands up and down her thighs before tugging her closer. She put her hands on my shoulders and eagerly accepted my kiss. The way she opened up, let me in, and gave me control had me holding her a little tighter. Delilah was too sweet for a man like me, too innocent.

When I broke the kiss, I knew exactly what I wanted. Her. In my bed, every fucking night. At least, until I knew for sure what I was feeling wasn't going to fade after a few days or weeks.

"Stay. Not just tonight, but tomorrow too."

"I didn't bring an overnight bag with me," she said.

"Text Missy a list of things you want, and I'll have a Prospect pick it up. Enough for a few days."

"You said tonight and tomorrow," she reminded me.

"Yeah, but I may want to keep you longer. Let's just leave it open-ended for now."

I was playing a dangerous game. As much as she fascinated me, I didn't think I'd want her to leave anytime soon. Once she realized I was planning to keep her indefinitely, she might decide she was finished with me. I had no doubt she could have any guy she wanted. I'd never met anyone sexier than her.

She gave a slight nod and a shy smile.

Little did she know tonight was only the beginning.

The nudge Barney gave me with his cold, wet nose said he was in complete agreement. She was ours and she wasn't going anywhere.

Chapter Four

Delilah

The President of Hades Abyss wanted me to stay at his house. It felt a little like I was living in a dream world. Men like him didn't keep women like me. Not for more than a night. Even then, I'd never had a guy of his caliber ever come onto me before. Part of me wondered if it had anything to do with me being a webcam girl. Had that wilder, naughtier side of me been what had snagged his attention?

He'd stepped outside to take a call, leaving me to wander his house. Barney followed at my heels. I'd been nosy and peeked inside the other rooms. The kitchen had a small round table and four chairs, and more counter space than I'd ever seen. I also found a walk-in pantry and laundry room. He had an office downstairs, small half-bath, and a decent-size dining room that didn't have so much as a chair in it. Upstairs, I found two empty rooms, and another he'd clearly set up for his grandkids. There was a toddler bed and crib in there, as well as toys, a changing table, and small dresser. I didn't think he looked old enough to be a grandfather.

I made my way back downstairs only to freeze partway down. Titan stood in the entryway, along with Missy and another man. I'd seen him once or twice and thought his name was Wizard. Missy looked a little pale and her hands trembled. I hurried down the steps, ready to give her my support. I didn't know what was going on, but she was clearly upset.

"Everything okay?" I asked.

"Not even fucking close," said Titan.

Barney barked and danced at my feet. I noticed he stayed between me and the others. Was he protecting me?

I glanced between Titan and Missy, then focused on the other guy. I'd been right. His name was Wizard. The patches on his cut said he was also the club Secretary. What on earth was going on? Why did Missy seem scared?

I reached for her hand, but Titan grabbed my arm and hauled me away from her. Barney growled, baring his teeth, as he glanced from Titan to Missy and back. I wasn't sure if he was going to bite Missy or the man holding my arm.

"Titan, what's going on?" I asked. "Did Missy do something wrong? Did I?"

"Oh, we'll get to you in a minute, sweetheart. Right now, Missy has some explaining to do," Titan said.

"You damn well knew who Shella was before you let her join your webcam girls," Wizard said, glaring at Missy. "We have no issues with the Devil's Fury, but if Grizzly finds out his daughter is one of your girls, all hell is going to break loose. And guess who he'll be coming for?"

"She's her own person," Missy said. "She's legally an adult. I ran a background check, just like I promised I would. It came back clean."

"Motherfucker," Wizard muttered. "If Outlaw runs across that shit, we're fucked. From now on, I do all the background checks. No one joins your little site unless I give the okay. You may have to comply with the FCC and all the laws that go with having that sort of website, but I can't have you bringing trouble through our doors."

Titan was staring at me, his eyes darker than before. The way his jaw clenched said I'd done something to piss him off. I just didn't know what.

"Shella is done," Wizard said. "I caught her doing far more than getting herself off on her spot tonight. She had two Prospects with her, and she did have the proper release forms, but it's going to make things a hundred times worse once someone recognizes her."

Whoa. Two men at once? Titan was the first guy I'd ever been with, and since he'd been far from small, I was a little sore. Shella was either braver than me, or far more experienced. I didn't really know her all that well. She hung out quite a bit with Missy and the other webcam girls. I'd never felt like I fit in with them. Even though Missy had been my friend since high school, it was clear she'd changed. I knew I wasn't exactly the same as I'd been before moving here, but the things I'd seen tonight, and heard about, made me feel like some innocent small-town girl.

Titan switched his gaze to Missy, and I felt like I could breathe again. I didn't like it when he stared me down like that. He was too intimidating.

Since she was here and getting chewed out, I was going to assume this meant I wasn't getting any of my stuff tonight. Did he even still want me to stay?

"Shella doesn't step foot on the compound again. If I find out she's still doing her show from a different location, you'll be finished here. Not just in our clubhouse, but the entire fucking town." Titan moved closer to her. "Nothing happens around here without me finding out. Now get the fuck out of my house. I need to have a chat with Delilah."

Wizard handed a file folder to Titan and then walked out with Missy on his heels. He shut the door, twisted the lock, then turned that terrifying gaze on me again. I felt like I would come out of my skin and needed to run away. I'd heard of a flight or fight response, but I'd never experienced it until now. And I definitely chose flight.

Titan smacked the folder against his thigh, then pointed to the stairs. I walked up them, my heart slamming against my ribs with every step. I stopped on the landing and he prodded me toward his room. Barney followed until Titan gave him the order to go lie down. His ears dropped and he went back to the stairs, then flopped on the floor by the top step.

"Get on the bed, Delilah," he said, his voice smoky with a hint of violence.

I whimpered and scurried onto the bed, wondering what I'd done. He hadn't hurt me so far and didn't seem like the type. What if I was wrong? I should have run out the door when I had the chance, even if I was only wearing his shirt. I stared at him, my stomach knotting as I wondered what he was going to do to me.

"Take off the shirt and toss it aside," he said.

My hands shook as I obeyed. A little voice in my head was screaming at me, calling me an idiot.

"Titan, what did I…"

He growled and advanced on me, reaching out to grip my hair in a tight fist. "What do you call me when it's just us?"

"Justin," I said. "What did I do?"

He tossed the folder onto the bed. "Know what that is?"

"N-No."

"Why the fuck didn't you tell me who your grandfather is?"

My brow furrowed. "My grandfather? Why does it matter who he is?"

Titan braced a knee on the bed and moved in closer. The scent of him teased my nose and I looked up, catching his gaze. His hold on my hair loosened even though he still had the tresses wrapped around his fingers.

"Baby, do you have any idea who Gregory Montcliff is?" he asked.

"My mom's father." I knew he had money, but he'd never discussed it with me. My mother hadn't liked him for the longest time, but he'd been good to his grandkids. She'd once told me how he'd planned for her to marry an old man, some rich guy her dad knew. Instead, she'd met my daddy and fallen in love.

"Your grandpa has been known to have shady dealings. In fact, he's being watched closely by the club down there, the Dixie Reapers. There used to be a rival club in the area, the Vipers. The Reapers ran them out and have been working on cleaning up the town. There's still drugs and whores, but they take out the trash when they're able."

"What does that have to do with my grandfather?" I asked

"No one has been able to dig up anything substantial yet, but the Dixie Reapers think his money might be coming from sales of… illegal items." He tipped my head back. "Like women."

It felt like the world came to a halt. My grandfather was selling women? Did that mean… Oh, God! My car. Had he paid for it at the expense of someone else's freedom? And what exactly did he mean by *selling women*? Brokering marriages? Or prostitution? My stomach twisted and gurgled. I felt the burn at the back of my throat from bile and knew I was close to throwing up.

Titan cupped my cheek and pressed his lips to mine. "Easy, baby. I shouldn't have told you like that. Should have waited to see what you knew. It's clear you had no idea."

I shook my head. "I didn't. I swear. But what did you mean he sells women?"

"He procures women for men like him. Wealthy. Older. Without any scruples whatsoever. Some marry them so it at least looks legit on paper. In all honesty, they're treated like garbage. He finds girls who have no hope, no money. Or preys on their families, promising large sums of cash in exchange for finding their daughters wealthy husbands." His lips pressed together. "Sometimes they aren't so lucky to even have the illusion of being married."

"I think I'm going to be sick," I murmured. "No wonder my mother hated him. She'd said he'd practically sold her to Thomas Kale III, but I had thought she was partially joking. Like maybe he was pushing her to marry the guy, but now I have to wonder if money really did exchange hands, or something else."

Oh, shit. Did my mother know? I didn't think she'd have let me accept the car if she'd known where the money came from. Or my dad either for that matter. I'd known how much he hated my grandfather, but I'd thought it was because he'd been from the wrong side of town.

"Justin, if he's really doing that, we have to stop him."

He ran his hand down my back, then pulled me closer. He wrapped me in his arms and pressed a kiss to the top of my head. "Not our fight, baby. He's in the

Dixie Reapers' territory, but I'll let them know they have our support if they need it."

"Why were you so angry with me?" I asked. "I thought… for a minute, I worried you might hurt me."

"No, baby. I might spank your ass, tie you up and make you beg me for it, but I'd never hit you. If your grandfather finds out you're here, and what you've been doing to earn a living, he could cause trouble for the club. Or try to."

My eyes went wide, and I pulled away from him. "Oh, God. What if he's seen me? Anyone could get access to the site. My grandfather. My brothers. My dad!"

Why hadn't I thought of that before? I'd just gone my merry way, doing whatever I wanted, and hadn't for one second thought of the repercussions. Anyone could access the site as long as they were old enough and had the money to pay for it. What had I done?

Titan gripped my chin and forced me to focus on him. "Only going to say this once, so listen carefully. No one has seen you but me. The moment I knew you were here to be a webcam girl, I had Wizard set it up so your feed goes straight to me and nowhere else. Made it look like you were getting hits from multiple sources, but you weren't. Your secret is safe."

I sagged against him, trying to process everything. My grandfather was a monster, and Titan had been watching me get off from the beginning. On the upside, he'd been the only one. "Why would you do that?"

"Because the thought of anyone seeing you like that infuriated me. All these curves are for my eyes only. I knew it then. Just didn't make my move yet. Thought you needed time. Missy made it sound like you'd never tasted freedom. I didn't want you to feel like I was shoving you in a cage."

It's exactly how I would have felt. Right now, I wasn't too sure if I liked the fact he wanted to keep me or if it scared the shit out of me. I'd never had a boyfriend. The last two months had been my only chance to live my life. My family had always watched me like a hawk, and it had been wonderful being out from under their scrutiny. Was I ready to give it all up just to be with Titan?

He was sexy. Had been sweet to me. Protective. I liked all those things about him. Would staying really be such a bad thing? Even if I gave up being a webcam girl, he'd been the one paying me all along. I doubted he'd ask me to be here with him, give up my job, and then refuse me the essentials I needed. I could always try to get a job in town to earn a little money of my own.

"Where do we go from here?" I asked.

He rubbed his thumb across my lower lip. "For starters, you're going to move your things here. You're mine, Delilah. Especially knowing who your grandfather is. If I let you go and something happened to you, I'd never forgive myself. You'll be in my bed every night. I'll be claiming you, officially, with my club."

"I'm not sure I know exactly what you mean by claiming me."

"You'd be my old lady. My woman. No one touches you and lives to talk about it. And you sure as hell don't let another man kiss you or fuck you. A lot of men in my position wouldn't offer the same in return, but I will. You're the only woman I want, Delilah. I told you we'd be monogamous, and I meant it. Think of it as the equivalent of being my wife, just without the paperwork."

Wife? The room spun a little. We barely knew one another, and he wanted to keep me... forever? Who did that sort of thing? It was insane to even consider it, and yet I had to admit I was tempted. No one had ever made me feel the way he did.

"And if I want to go visit my family?"

"I'd rather you wait until things are sorted where your grandfather is concerned, but I won't keep you from your family. You want to see them, I'll arrange for it to happen. They can come here, or I'll send men with you if I can't take you myself."

"And if I don't want to stay? What if I think all this is completely insane and I want to leave?" I asked.

He held me tighter. The set of his jaw, the flash in his eyes, all told me he didn't plan to let me go. The way he'd made my body sing, I knew if he tied me to the bed like he'd threatened it wouldn't be long before he had me agreeing to anything he wanted. What would my mother say?

I wanted to talk to her. Needed to. Before I did or said anything else, I needed to hear her voice of reason. If she told me I needed to run, then I would. Somehow.

"Can I have a minute? And a phone?" He looked like he might argue so I cut off any objection he could have. "I need to talk to my mom. Please, Justin."

"Fine. You can use my cell phone. I'll give you ten minutes, then I'ın coming back." He released me, stood, and handed me the phone. With one last look, he left, shutting the door behind him.

I breathed a sigh of relief, noting my fingers trembled as I dialed my mom's number. It was really early in the morning. There was a chance she wouldn't answer. Even if she did, I didn't think her or my dad would be too pleased at being woken up at a little after midnight.

"Someone better be dying." I winced at the growl in my dad's voice. It figured he'd answer even though I'd called my mom's cell phone.

"Hi, Daddy. Can I talk to Mom?"

I heard the rustle of sheets. "Delilah? Whose phone are you on? What's wrong?"

"Nothing's wrong. I need some advice from Mom, that's all."

"Answer me. Who the fuck's phone are you using?" he demanded.

"Titan's. He's the President of the Hades Abyss MC, and before you say anything, he's not a bad guy. He's been good to me, Daddy."

I heard my mother talking in the background, then what sounded like a struggle. When she came on the line, I could hear the irritation in her voice and hoped it wasn't directed at me. As much as I hated to disappoint my dad, having my mom mad at me was even worse.

"What's going on, Delilah?" she asked.

"I've met someone. He wants me to move in." I swallowed hard. "Actually, he wants more than that and I don't know what to do. It's too fast, isn't it?"

I heard more rustling, then a door shutting. "We're taking this elsewhere."

Great. It wasn't like my dad wouldn't pry it out of her the second she hung up. All she'd done was delay the inevitable. I heard the creak of her favorite wooden rocking chair and knew she'd gone to the living room.

"Now tell me about this man," she said.

"He goes by Titan and he's the President of the Hades Abyss MC." I licked my lips, waiting on her to say something, but she didn't. "He's been good to me. Protective. Sweet. He says he wants to claim me. That it's like being his wife without the paperwork. It's crazy to even consider it, isn't it?"

My mom snorted. "Delilah, did I ever tell you how I met your father?"

I knew she'd broken down and Dad had come to her rescue. She'd never really given any details, but now I was curious. "Not everything. Just that he helped you."

"Oh, he helped me all right," she said. "Right out of my panties."

I gasped and nearly dropped the phone. I might have had a lot of conversations with my mother over the years, but we usually avoided any sort of sex talk when it came to her and my dad. "Mom!"

"It's true. I'd never met anyone like him before. We hadn't even known each other more than two days before he whisked me off to Vegas and married me. So, I may not be the best person to ask if you're wanting someone to tell you *not* to move in with Titan."

I didn't even know what to say.

"Delilah, no one knows your heart except you. Do you love him or think you can?" she asked.

It was too soon to love him. Even though we'd spoken, we hadn't really gotten to know one another all that well. You couldn't love a stranger, right? But... Yes, there was a chance I *could* love him. "I think I could."

"Just follow your heart. As long as you're happy, that's all that matters. Well, happy and safe."

"I am, Mom. He'd never do anything to hurt me." I might not know a lot about Titan, but that was one thing I felt all the way to my soul. Yes, I'd been worried earlier when he'd been so angry. Then he'd sworn he'd never hit me, and I believed him. I didn't know why, just that I did.

"Whatever you decide, you have my support," she said. "Your father, on the other hand... Well, he won't be too happy about it. Neither will your brothers, but they'll all get over it. Do what you need to do in order to be happy, Delilah. We love you and only want the best for you. If that's Titan, then grab hold and never let go."

"Love you, Mom."

She blew me a kiss and hung up. I set the phone on the bedside table, pulled Titan's shirt back on, and went to find him. I didn't see him upstairs and made my way down to the living room. It was empty so I kept searching, finally finding him in his office.

Barney lay on the floor and leapt up when he saw me, racing to my side with a happy grin on his face. I knelt and petted him, getting a few kisses in thanks.

"Get everything squared away?" he asked.

"Yeah. I just needed to talk things out, and my mom has always been there for me. I knew she'd have some advice for me."

"And?"

"I want to stay, to give us a chance. I'm scared, Justin. I've never been in a relationship before and I have no idea if I'm even capable of it. If you claim me, and it's a forever kind of thing, what happens if everything goes to hell? What if we fight and can't stand one another after a few days or weeks?"

Titan pushed his chair back and motioned for me to come closer. When I reached his side, he tugged me down onto his lap. "Baby, I don't make rash decisions. I've watched you, and not just on your webcam show. You're sweet, sexy, and I've never wanted anyone the way I want you, Delilah. It hasn't died down over the two months I've known you, and I don't think it ever will. If you want to stay a few days and see how it goes, I'll give you that."

"A few days?" I asked.

"It will give you a chance to see what it would be like to live with me. I'm waiting on two of my guys to come back from a run. After they get back, I'll be calling Church, and I'll officially claim you unless you've decided to leave by then."

It was better than no time at all, but still… a few days to decide the rest of my life? It felt like I was standing at the edge of a cliff. If I made the wrong choice, I could fall to my death. Then again, maybe if I took the leap, I wouldn't fall. I'd fly.

"All right. A few days."

He put his hand on the back of my neck and drew me closer, then kissed the hell out of me. I didn't know what I'd just gotten myself into, but I hoped it was the beginning of my happily-ever-after.

Chapter Five

Titan

The sun peeked through the blinds and bathed Delilah in a soft, golden glow. She'd been here three days. I always found her beautiful, but with her hair spread across my pillows, she was even more stunning. I knew I needed to get up and deal with club business, but I wanted to linger a little longer. Reaching out, I ran my fingers over her cheek. After weeks of wanting her in my bed, she was finally here, right where she belonged. Not having been around clubs before, especially like the Hades Abyss, I knew me wanting to claim her so soon after meeting her had to have been a shock. I'd known men who took old ladies within a day or two of meeting them, so two months seemed like forever to me. Sometimes you just knew when someone was meant to be yours.

Hell, even Barney knew she was ours. He'd taken to following her all over the house, barely leaving her side. I had to kick his ass out at night and shut the door, otherwise he'd probably try to bite my dick off when I fucked Delilah. The dog was smart, but if he thought she was being hurt, I had no doubts whatsoever he'd protect her. Even if it meant biting the hand that fed him.

I cursed when my phone rang, and I grabbed it before the noise woke Delilah. She hadn't gotten much sleep and I knew she had to be exhausted. The screen flashed with *Boomer* and I answered.

"What the fuck do you want, asshole?" I asked my VP.

"I know you've got your woman there and I hate to interrupt, but some shit's going down and needs your attention."

Fucking hell. "What now? Wizard already told me about Delilah's family. And one of the webcam girls being the daughter of Grizzly. What the fuck else could go wrong? Is it too much to ask that we have a quiet fucking week every now and then?"

Boomer cleared his throat. "Well, since you asked. Shella is gone. Not like gone from the clubhouse, but as in she left town entirely. The two prospects who tag-teamed her were Owen and Riley. Even though they were dumbasses, they didn't break any rules."

"What the fuck do you mean she's gone?" I asked.

"Packed up her shit and left. Missy gave her some cash until the girl gives her a forwarding address for her final check. Not sure where she's going to end up."

"That it?" I asked. On the upside, maybe the Devil's Fury wouldn't come knocking at our door looking for her. At the same time, I didn't like keeping shit from Grizzly. I'd have to let the man know his daughter had been here. Probably leave out the part of her being a webcam girl, or the fact she'd screwed any guy who'd looked her way while she'd been here. What a fucking mess!

"Not quite. The shipment we were expecting is late. Sent Morgan and Galahad out to check on it. That was an hour ago. Haven't heard from them and they aren't back yet. Brick and Smoke came back from their run without issue. Already handed the cash over to Pretty Boy so it can be put into the right accounts."

I knew exactly which shipment he meant. I'd not wanted to make the deal with a bunch of mobsters, but I hadn't exactly had much choice. There was one thing I'd never allow and that was for anyone to abuse women. If that meant I had to purchase their freedom, then so be it. The fact I'd just bought three women from a Bratva brothel, and they were now gone along with my men, didn't bode well.

"See if Wizard can track them. I'll throw some clothes on and head to the clubhouse."

Boomer snorted. "No offense, Pres, but you probably smell like pussy. At least shower first."

I'd have flipped him off if he could see me. "Never bothered you before."

"Yeah, well. It's different when you smell like a club whore. Don't think you want everyone smelling your old lady on you."

"Not officially my old lady," I said, glancing at Delilah.

"Maybe not on the record yet, but she's yours. Everyone here knows it."

"Pull everyone who isn't missing, including Prospects. For once, we're bringing them into Church. Need all hands on deck for this one. I have a feeling those fuckers have double-crossed us, and likely have our men tied up somewhere if they haven't outright killed them."

"Only if they want to start a war," Boomer said.

"Doubt they care either way."

I disconnected the call and went to shower. After a quick scrubbing, I got out and dried off, then dressed as quick as I could. I leaned over the bed to press a kiss to Delilah's cheek. I hated leaving her, especially while she was asleep. I pulled a small notepad from the bedside table drawer and a pen so I could scribble her a note, letting her know where I was. When I was finished, I put on my boots and headed out, stopping long enough to let Barney out to pee and back inside again.

Any other time, I'd have left someone outside my house to keep an eye on her. Since no one outside the compound knew she was mine, she should be safe enough for now. Not to mention Barney would bite anyone who tried to hurt Delilah. Our chapter was still on the small side, but the trouble that kept landing at our feet meant we needed more men. We'd added three Prospects since the incident with my daughter, especially since we'd patched in Sean, who now went by Galahad.

I knew some thought I'd patched him out of pity. His cousin, MaryAnne, had been snatched, and abused horribly. It had taken a long time to track her down and save her, although, I wasn't too sure there'd been much left to save. The sweet teenager he'd known was long gone, leaving only a shell behind. Under constant care at a private mental facility, MaryAnne had everything she could possibly need. It wasn't enough. I'd failed her.

Since bringing her home, I'd made it my mission to save as many women as I could. Those who chose prostitution were another matter, unless they'd decided they wanted out. The women who came to the clubhouse, the ones we called club whores, were there voluntarily. They knew the score. In exchange for being easy pussy to anyone in a cut, they got free drinks, recreational drugs if they so desired, and had a good time. Any who thought they'd get claimed were soon set straight on the matter.

I pulled up to the clubhouse and parked near the stairs. No matter how packed the lot became, I'd always have a spot reserved as President. Boomer had a place on the opposite side that was always left open for him. It looked like everyone was here already, or some had possibly never left. Wouldn't be the first time a few men had fallen asleep either in the rooms down the hall or slumped over the bar or tables.

I pushed open the doors and went inside, my eyes adjusting to the dim interior. Two barely clad women were asleep at the nearest table. The rest of the main room was empty. I made my way down the hall to Church and claimed my spot at the table. Not only was every patched brother at the table, except for those out on jobs, but the Prospects lined the wall.

"You're probably wondering why I called in everyone," I said. "Trouble has found us again, and I need every damn one of you. The shipment we were expecting is missing, along with some of our men. Wizard, were you able to pinpoint a location?"

He had his laptop open and tapped away at the keys a moment. "Their phones are all pinging from the same location, which is in the middle of nowhere. If we sent someone to retrieve them, I'm guessing they'd find the phones on the side of the road. The bikes are another matter."

"Wait. Bikes?" Philly asked. "What the fuck, Pres? You chipped our bikes?"

"After the things we've been through the last few years, yes. I had Wizard put a tracker on everyone's bikes." I'd also had him include one inside the lining of each officer's cut, but I wasn't about to share that. We'd had a rat in our midst before and I wasn't going to chance that information getting into the wrong hands. It could mean the difference in one of us coming home alive or in a body bag. "We're brothers. Family. And I will be damned if I'm ever leaving a man behind. If that means I put trackers on you or your bikes, then so be it. Don't like it? You know where the fucking door is."

Philly held up his hands. "Not trying to start shit, Titan. Just would have been nice to know."

"In case you're wondering, I used only the best money can buy, which means they're damn hard to discover. Unless they have state of the art equipment, the trackers go undetected, which is what we were counting on," Wizard said. "Actually, it's the brainchild of Wire and Lavender. The Dixie Reapers will be using them as well, if they aren't already."

"Nothing quite like having a leash shoved up your ass," Stone muttered. "I can see why you'd feel it was necessary, but I don't like it."

"The location of the bikes?" I asked, needing Wizard to focus and get back on track.

"About fifteen miles outside of town. Looks like a warehouse complex. Getting an exact location would be a bit harder. Might have to send in a few men for recon, figure out exactly where they're being held and what we're up against," Wizard said.

"Any volunteers?" I asked.

"I'll go," said Pretty Boy.

Poison and Gravel both raised their hands. Before I asked if anyone else wanted to go, two Prospects volunteered as well.

"Count me in," Riley said.

"And me," said one of the newer Prospects, Cache.

"All right. Pretty Boy, since you're an officer, I'm putting you in charge. I want you to roll out within the hour, but don't go in guns blazing. We need methodical and not maniacal."

"Which is why I'm staying here," Boomer said. He grinned and I flipped him off, although he wasn't wrong. He'd earned his name by blowing shit up.

"Just one other matter of business before everyone leaves. I'm claiming Delilah. As of now, she's officially my old lady, which means you'll give her the respect she deserves," I said.

"She know about you paying to see her webcam show?" Wizard asked.

"I told her. I think she actually felt relieved. When she realized her family could have stumbled across the site, she seemed embarrassed. There's some shit we'll need to discuss about her family, but I want this other issue settled first. Everyone get the fuck out." I slammed my fist on the table and stood.

Wizard hung back and approached after everyone else had left. He handed me a flash drive and without a word, walked out. I closed my fist around it, then shoved it into my pocket. Whatever was on it, I doubted it was something good. I'd open the file or files when I had a moment alone.

Before I went home, I rode to the nearest bakery and got a sack of kolaches. No doubt Delilah would be hungry when she woke up, and I knew I was damn well starving. I'd have gotten a box of donuts, but I knew they wouldn't travel well in my saddlebags. I stashed the kolaches, then headed back to the compound.

The house was still silent when I got home. I put the food on the kitchen table, then went up to find Delilah. I smiled when I saw her curled around my pillow, the sheet around her ankles. She'd twisted and turned until my shirt had ridden up to her waist, exposing her sexy ass. It was tempting as hell to crawl back into bed with her, but I knew if I did, I'd want to do far more than wake her up.

Barney lay at her feet, his head on his paws. He eyed me but didn't budge.

I placed a knee on the mattress and ran my fingers through her hair. "Wake up, beautiful. Time for breakfast."

She murmured and squeezed her eyes shut tighter. Cute as hell. I leaned down and kissed her cheek before I licked the shell of her ear. She moaned and turned her lips toward me. I couldn't resist and claimed a morning kiss.

Her eyes slowly opened. "Morning."

"I have breakfast downstairs. Hungry?"

Her stomach growled and her cheeks turned pink. I helped her from the bed, fighting to keep my hands off her ass or anywhere else that would land us right back under the covers. Instead, I herded her to the bathroom so she could take care of her morning business, then led her downstairs to the kitchen. The click of Barney's nails let me know he'd followed. I didn't see him at first, then realized he'd settled under the table right at Delilah's feet. It seemed I no longer had a dog. My woman had stolen him without even trying.

The kolaches were still warm and I plated two for each of us. There were more in the bag if that wasn't enough. No matter how much Barney begged, he wouldn't get one. At least, not by my hand. The vet had warned against giving him people food, and he was on a special diet of expensive dog food.

"I may have to step out again later. Club business," I said.

She took a bite of her breakfast and eyed me but didn't say anything. I wasn't sure what I'd expected. Any other woman would probably have asked what I'd be doing or where I'd be going. Not Delilah. She wasn't like anyone I'd ever met before.

"Not even curious?" I asked.

"Would it do me any good? According to Missy, you guys never discuss club business around anyone."

"She's right. We don't. I'm just surprised you didn't at least attempt to get anything out of me."

She leaned back in her chair. "I have three brothers and an overprotective dad. Trust me. I know when a man doesn't want to tell me something, especially if he thinks it's for my own good, that I won't be able to pull the information from him no matter what I try. No sense making you mad or giving myself a headache over it."

"I think you're going to settle in here just fine." I winked at her. "And for the record, I'm not keeping things from you because I think it will keep you safe. If you're in danger, I'll tell you. This shit I'm dealing with today doesn't have anything to do with you, or my daughter."

She sat up a little straighter. "There's another woman here? I mean, other than the ones who party at the clubhouse? Your daughter lives here at the compound?"

I nodded. "She's Kraken's old lady and they have a house inside the gates. Her name's Phoebe."

She opened and shut her mouth. "You mentioned being a grandpa, and you said your daughter was with Kraken, even mentioned he'd brought her home, but I didn't realize their home was at the compound. Will I get to meet them?"

"You will. After I get things situated today, I'll give Kraken a call and have him bring everyone over for dinner. We can order pizza or Chinese. The kids are too small to eat either. Or rather, Phoebe refuses to let Ember eat either one. I can understand the Chinese since she might choke on it, but pizza?" I shook my head. "Every kid should be allowed to have it."

"How old is Ember?" she asked.

"Around two. I don't know her exact age. Only my daughter tells the kids' ages in months. Far as I'm concerned, you're either one age or another. Who the fuck measures their life in months?"

She raised her eyebrows. "You don't know how old your grandkids are?"

I shrugged. "I can tell you the date of anything going on with the club. But birthdays? Someone will have to remind me."

She let the matter go, but I couldn't tell if it bothered her or amused her. I'd have to find out when her birthday was and put it in the calendar in my phone. Something told me if I forgot my woman's birthday, she'd have my balls. She might be all sweetness and innocence, but I had no doubt she'd stand toe to toe with me if the need arose. I didn't want a pushover for my old lady. I had no idea how she'd react if she saw a club whore trying to get into my pants. Part of me wanted to find out, but at the same time, I didn't want to upset her. There was no competition whatsoever, as the only woman I wanted was sitting across from me right now.

"Why don't you call Missy and have her bring your things over? You have to be tired of running around in my shirts. I know we've been a bit preoccupied, but you should at least get anything you need immediately. Someone can get the bags or boxes from her at the gate or clubhouse and drop them by the house. I'd prefer that she not come here."

"Why not?" she asked.

"She came with Wizard about an issue with the club and her business. That's not the same as her bringing stuff to the house for you. If she's permitted to come hang out whenever she wants, she may think she holds more power in the club than she does. I know the two of you are friends, but you're mine now, Delilah, and that means people will use you to get to me, or to gain an advantage with the Hades Abyss. Missy doesn't just run her business out of her clubhouse, but she parties there too."

She chewed on her lip and seemed to think it over. "I can understand why you'd feel she might do that. She's not the same person she was before. There's nothing wrong with that. It's just that she seems a little like a stranger some days. I'm not sure I know this new version very well."

"I need to go handle a few things before I head out. Why don't you call Missy about your stuff? You can use my phone. I want you to settle in a bit while I'm gone today. You can change anything you want, as long as you keep out of my office."

She gave a quick nod and I slid my phone across the table to her. While she was occupied, I went to my office and pulled the flash drive from my pocket. I plugged it into the computer and pulled up the files. The one labeled *MaryAnne* made me pause. I clicked it, and immediately silenced the sound while I tried to get the volume adjusted. It looked like they'd wrapped her in a straitjacket while she screamed and thrashed. I hadn't realized those were even still in use. What the fuck was going on?

I went through a few more clips and realized quickly MaryAnne was being abused. It pissed me the fuck off, especially after all she'd suffered already. We'd been led to believe she was nearly catatonic. It didn't seem to be the case. I had to get her out of there, even if I didn't know where to put her. Galahad still stayed in a room at the clubhouse while his home was being built. I'd talk to Boomer and see if we could figure something out.

The other files contained more information on Delilah's family. It looked like her brothers had lived a fairly clean life. Her dad had done a little jail time way back when, but not for anything serious. It looked like his business was doing well, and he hadn't caused any trouble since he'd married Delilah's mom. I pulled up my email and shot off a message to Wizard. *I need everything you've got on MaryAnne.*

I'd failed her twice now. I refused to let it happen again.

Chapter Six

Delilah

A Prospect had dropped my things off at Titan's house. My phone was tucked in a box along with my purse and other essentials. Missy had shoved some clothes into two plastic bags. I knew I had a lot more at the apartment, but this would do for now. My phone still had a charge, even though it was nearly dead. The missed calls and texts weren't a good sign.

Dad: *Where the fuck are you? Answer your phone!*
Mom: *We're worried. Call us!*

Each sent at least a half-dozen messages like the first, and my brothers had even sent a handful. It looked like they'd all tried to call me nearly every hour today and a few times last night. Even though I'd spoken to Mom, the conversation I'd had with her had seemed to only make things worse. I should have known to check in. I hadn't gone more than a day without calling or texting since I'd moved here.

I set up a group text with all of them and quickly typed out a message. *I'm fine. Forgot to charge my phone.*

It wasn't entirely a lie. I really did need to charge it. I pulled my cord and block from the box and plugged it into the nearest outlet. It would take at least an hour to get half my battery life back. I dug out the rest of the items and put them away, leaving the clothes for last. He'd said I could move things, but I felt awkward pawing through his drawers to make space. Instead, I set those items aside and hung up the two dresses Missy had packed. I could deal with the rest later.

Titan had a small TV on his dresser, and I switched it on. Since I'd plugged my phone in here, I didn't want to wander far. My family was sure to respond soon, and they'd just worry again if they couldn't reach me. I flipped through the channels until I found a movie I'd seen a hundred times, then settled back against the pillows on the bed. Barney lay at the side of the bed. I'd never had a dog before, and I'd fallen for him quickly.

My phone started chirping with texts. I let it go a few minutes, then scrolled through to read them all. If I tried to answer separately, it would take forever. Instead, I tried to compile everything into one message.

I'm moving out of the apartment. I'll send you my new address tomorrow or day after. Everything is fine. No, you don't need to come get me. No, you don't need to kick anyone's ass, but thanks for offering. I'm tired. I'll call later.

I set the phone back down and watched the movie, doing my best to ignore the non-stop messages coming through from my family. After ten minutes of the stupid phone going off, I silenced it. I knew they'd want to know why I was moving and where. Which would mean I'd have to tell them about Titan, and I had no idea how to explain him to my family. Mom knew a little, but not everything. I wasn't sure I wanted to share *everything* for that matter. I'd never mentioned him during my previous phone calls since moving here, even though we'd met two months ago, and I saw him on a regular basis when I'd come in for work. I was also a little concerned how they'd handle the age gap. It didn't bother *me*, but my family was another matter. I knew my dad was older than my mom. My brothers had often dated women younger than me. I also knew it would be different when it was their sister or daughter in the relationship.

One movie ended up being two before I heard the door slam shut downstairs. I started to get up and go see if Titan was all right, but I heard more banging.

At one point, it almost sounded like he'd started tossing furniture around. My throat tightened and my stomach knotted. What if it wasn't Titan downstairs? He'd said I'd be safe here, and I'd felt safe.

Heavy steps came up the stairs and I felt like locking the door. If it *was* Titan, he'd probably be pissed if I locked him out of his own room. I watched and waited. When I saw him at the top of the landing, I breathed a sigh of relief. The tension in his shoulders and the way his hands were clenched would have been enough to tell me he was pissed, if I hadn't already heard all the noise downstairs.

He stopped just inside the bedroom doorway.

"Are you all right?" I asked.

"No. Not even fucking close."

I got up and went to him, reaching up to cup his cheek. "Can I help?"

"No one can help. I fucked up and it's cost the club. Galahad is nearly dead, and so is the Prospect who went with him. The girls we were trying to save were slaughtered right in front of us."

I didn't even know what to say. I leaned against him, wanting to offer him comfort. The brutality of what he described was beyond anything I could comprehend. I knew there was ugliness in the world, but I'd never experienced it myself, and I hoped I never did. I took his hand and led him into the bathroom, then I turned on the shower, letting the water get good and hot.

Titan stared at the wall, unmoving.

I gently removed his cut and set it on the counter before helping him out of the rest of his clothes. I gave him a nudge into the shower and leaned up to kiss his cheek, not caring if the shower spray got my shirt damp.

"Let the water wash it away, Justin. You can't change what's happened. Let it all out and when you're done, I'll have a surprise for you in the kitchen. We'll sit down and maybe we can come up with some ideas to at least help those who were injured." I ran my hand down his arm. "I may not know a lot about your world, but I'm here. In whatever way you need me."

I moved away and shut the glass door, then hurried downstairs. I'd browsed the cabinets and fridge earlier and knew there wasn't a lot to work with, but he did have some box mixes for cakes and brownies. They were probably for when his family came over. Mid-reach, I stopped. His family. I rushed back up the stairs and got his phone. What had he said? His daughter was with someone named… Kraken? I took the phone to the kitchen with me and found the name under his contacts.

"You need me, Pres?" the man asked the second the call connected.

"Um, it's not Titan. It's Delilah."

"Everything all right?" he asked, sounding more alert than before.

"No. I don't think so. Titan is… what happened today hit him hard. I was going to make some brownies, but I think he could use his family right now."

"I'll get my wife and kids. We'll be there in ten minutes." He paused. "Thanks for calling, Delilah. I think you'll be good for him."

That remained to be seen. He could be pissed as hell when he found out what I'd done. I mixed the brownies and popped them into the oven. I set the timer, then went to the living room to find a family friendly movie I thought little kids might like. *Wizard of Oz*? No, the witch might be scary to little Ember.

Charlotte's Web? Probably not. Even I cried when Charlotte died. I finally found an animated *Scooby Doo* movie and put that on. Who didn't like a big goofy Great Dane?

The front door opened, and a man came in, a little girl clutched in his arms, and a pretty woman behind him with a baby. My hands shook a little as nerves hit me hard. I was meeting Titan's family. What if they didn't like me?

Kraken came into the living room and set Ember down. The little girl gave me a curious look before focusing on the TV. She plopped on the floor and stuck her thumb in her mouth. Barney scampered into the room and stretched out next to the little girl.

"You must be Delilah," Kraken said, holding out his hand.

I shook it and cast a quick glance at his wife before looking at him again. Even though he was part of the club, I seldom saw him at the clubhouse the times I'd come in to work. It made me wonder if he avoided the place since he had a family at home waiting for him. Would Titan still go there at night? Would he party like he had before? He'd said he'd be faithful, and I didn't think he'd lied to me, but I wasn't sure how to feel about him being around all those naked women.

"So you're the woman my dad decided to keep?" the woman asked. Her lips were pursed, and her eyebrows raised, as if she couldn't believe he'd want someone like me. I tugged at my shirt, wishing it didn't hug my belly quite so much. When she suddenly smiled and laughed, I jolted. "I'm glad to meet you. I'm Phoebe."

"Um, hi." I glanced between her and her husband again, wondering if I was about to be the butt of a joke.

"Sorry about that," Phoebe said. "I shouldn't have tried to make you feel bad. Honestly, I'm thrilled he found someone."

"It doesn't bother you that I'm close to your age?" I asked.

Phoebe shook her head. "Nope. Kraken is just two years younger than my dad. I can't exactly say anything without being a hypocrite now, can I?"

No, when she put it that way, she certainly couldn't. Her warm smile set me at ease, and I began to relax. I focused on the little bundle in her arms, moving a bit closer to peer at the baby. He was so cute!

"This is Banner," she said. "And Ember is the one you won't be able to pry away from the TV until that movie goes off."

I heard footsteps on the stairs. My heart slammed against my ribs as I worried over Titan's reaction. I'd told him I'd have a surprise in the kitchen. He'd no doubt thought I meant food, and I had, but it just seemed like as bad a day as he'd had his family might be what he needed more than sugar.

He came into the room in just his jeans and barefoot. Liquid heat pooled inside me, even as I watched him anxiously for any sort of reaction. He looked at each of his family members before swinging his gaze my way, both eyebrows arched.

"I, um… I thought maybe you'd like to see your family, since you'd had a bad day and all." I chewed my lower lip. "I also have brownies baking."

Titan shook Kraken's hand, hugged his daughter, kissed his grandson, then pulled me against his chest. I felt his lips brush the top of my head.

"Thank you," he murmured.

I nodded against him, wrapping my arms around his waist. The timer went off in the kitchen and I pulled away so I could rescue the brownies from burning. I set them on the counter to cool. I hadn't thought to ask about any allergies and wished I'd been able to make a second dessert just in case. The brownies had walnuts. Since Titan had purchased them, I had to hope that meant they were safe for his family to eat.

I took down some small plates, grabbed a handful of forks, and got a knife out to cut the brownies. Titan didn't have a trivet so I used a kitchen towel to place under the brownie pan and put it in the center of the kitchen table. Then I set everything else out so everyone could help themselves. I waited a few minutes, letting the brownies cool a little more and giving Titan some time to talk to Kraken and Phoebe, then I called them into the kitchen.

Ember clung to Titan as he came through the doorway. My ovaries exploded at the sight of him holding the little girl, and I wondered if he wanted more children. We hadn't discussed it, or much of anything. Well, nothing we *should* be talking about. Life-changing things couples should know before deciding to live together forever. Those things we'd avoided. It was stupid to rush into a relationship with him, not knowing if we wanted the same things. And yet, all the man had to do was touch me, or give me that sexy wink, and I turned into a brainless puddle of hormones.

"I made the brownies with walnuts. I'm not sure if everyone can eat them," I said.

"We can pick out the nuts for Ember," Phoebe said. "I don't want to take a chance on her choking, but she won't eat more than a bite or two anyway."

"I'm the youngest of four siblings, so I'm afraid I haven't been around babies. None of my brothers have settled down yet," I said.

Phoebe gave her father a sly look. "Maybe there will be more babies here soon."

Titan choked on the bite he'd just taken. "Are you pregnant again already?"

Kraken snorted. "I think she meant you and Delilah."

Phoebe smiled at her husband and he looked like he might panic for a moment. Then she burst out laughing. "Oh, my God. Your face! No, I'm not pregnant, but I do want at least one more baby. Just not right this minute. I need some time to… I'm still grieving. I'm not ready for a third baby, but I do want one someday."

Titan didn't say anything, and he didn't so much as look my way. Did that mean he didn't want more kids? I could understand. His daughter was already an adult and had kids of her own. I didn't know how I felt about the possibility of never having kids. It wasn't something I'd planned in my immediate future, but I'd always thought I'd have one or two at some point in my life.

"Speaking of babies, did you hear Rocket and Violeta had a little boy? And Slider and Vasha are expecting," Kraken said.

I had no idea who those people were. They obviously didn't live here, since Titan had said Phoebe was the only other woman. I wondered if they were part of another club. With names like Slider and

Rocket, it seemed like they were bikers, like Titan and Kraken... unless their mothers really didn't like them.

"Well, your brothers need to get to work finding decent women and starting families," Phoebe said. "It would be nice for the kids to have someone to play with."

"I know a few who wouldn't mind settling down," Titan said, "but most are enjoying their freedom. They'll eventually tire of the scene at the clubhouse."

Everyone finished off the brownies and I started cleaning up. Barney pawed at my foot. I looked down and he gave a little bark before running to the back door. Since Titan was talking to his family, I let the dog out and stood on the back steps waiting for him. He raced around the yard, doing three laps, before putting his nose to the ground and sniffing out a spot. After he'd peed at least three times, barked at what seemed to be nothing at all, then sniffed the grass another ten minutes, I let him back inside.

Titan sat at the kitchen table and the house was quiet. I looked around and didn't even see signs we'd ever had visitors. Had they left while I'd been gone? I knew it was rude to not have said goodbye, but I'd invited them over to help Titan deal with his shitty day. The fact he'd smile and laughed meant I'd accomplished my goal, at least as long as they'd been here.

"Did they leave already?" I asked.

"Yeah. Ember was getting tired so they headed home to put the kids to bed." He held out his hand and I went to him. Titan pulled me down onto his lap. "Thank you. I don't know how you knew exactly what I needed, but I appreciate it."

"I may not know how all this works yet, but I'm pretty sure any relationship requires a bit of give and take. You needed me, so I helped in the only way I knew how. I can't make what happened go away, but I can at least give you a bit of comfort and help you de-stress, or try at any rate."

He hugged me tight. "I'm glad you walked into the club that day. I think Fate put you in my path. Knew I'd need you. I know shit won't be easy, and we're bound to fight at times. I can promise I'll never hurt you, not intentionally."

"So we should be completely honest with each other, right?" I asked.

"Of course. Do you think I've lied to you about something?" he asked.

"No. More like there are a lot of things we haven't discussed. Claiming me is your version of a marriage, if I understand correctly. You said we're exclusive. And it's a forever kind of thing."

"Right."

"We haven't talked about whether or not you want kids. You asked if I was on birth control, and you didn't exactly seem excited about the idea of a baby when Phoebe teased you about it earlier. Do you not want more children? I can understand if that's the case, since you have a grown daughter and grandkids."

He ran his hand up and down my thigh. "I haven't given it a lot of thought. I asked about birth control because right now, no, I don't think I want a baby. It doesn't mean I won't ever want one. I love my family, and the thought of raising a kid with you isn't unpleasant. There's just a lot of shit going on with the club. I'm not sure I have the time for an infant right now."

Well, it wasn't an outright no. I could live with that. For now. I leaned against him, cuddling closer. I didn't exactly want a baby right this second either. I just wanted to know there was a chance we could have one at a later time. He'd been great with Ember. There were plenty of men in the world who should have never been fathers. Titan wasn't one of them. Any kid he had would be lucky to have him for a dad.

Chapter Seven

Titan

I'd left Delilah asleep in our bed at dawn this morning. She'd been here nearly two weeks, and I still found it hard to walk away from her. I'd never met a more tempting woman. Just the right amount of innocent and naughty.

It was now closing in on noon and I hadn't even begun to dig my way through the pile of shit on my desk. The girls we'd lost still bothered me and would for a long time to come. I needed to know what went wrong. They'd agreed to sell those girls to us. So why kill them? If they were dead, they didn't earn any money. I hated that we still hadn't learned anything new.

I'd put in a call about the girls this morning. So far, my connection hadn't gotten back to me. I hoped that didn't mean he was buried six feet under. It should have been simple enough. We paid for the girls, brought them here, and it was done. Instead, everything had gone to shit. Those poor women had been slaughtered as if they meant nothing. Less than nothing. And my men…

As far as Bones could tell, they were both going to pull through, but it would be a hard road for them. Galahad had been especially fucked up. The club's connections had only gotten us so far, but I'd donated a fuck ton of money to the local hospital to grease the wheels a bit. He'd needed surgery to repair some of the damage, and I needed them to not ask questions, or bring in the police. It had put a dent in the club's accounts, but it was worth it.

There was a knock at the door, then my VP stepped into my office. "You got a minute?"

"If it involves more paperwork, or trouble, then no. Consider me on vacation in a remote place where no one can find me."

He snorted. "Yeah right. You could move to the moon and we'd find you."

I flipped him off, but the asshole only grinned.

"It's about your woman's family. We got some movement this morning. At some point, she must have called and talked to them, let them know where she was and who she was with," Boomer said.

"What brought you to that conclusion?" I asked. And yes, she'd called them.

"When you found out who he was, I called in a favor," Boomer said. "I asked some of the Dixie Reapers to keep an eye on things down that way. The grandfather in particular. Seems he was already on their radar, but they're being extra vigilant now. About two hours ago, he showed up at the parents' house. Looked pissed as fuck. When he left, he was on the phone."

"And that seems suspicious because..."

"Wire and Lavender hacked Gregory Montcliff's accounts, emails, and anything else they could get their fingers on. Seems there was a contract for Delilah to marry, and I use the term loosely, an acquaintance of Gregory's. Guy is loaded. Has houses in three US cities and two overseas. Money changed hands, and now he doesn't have Delilah to hand over. To say Grandpa is pissed is an understatement."

Jesus. I couldn't catch a damn break.

"I also asked them to look into that other issue. MaryAnne. You were right. She's being abused. The video we saw was just the beginning. It wasn't a one-time thing but ongoing, and it gets worse. Poor thing is scared of her own shadow by this point. Galahad is in no shape to go get her. You want to send anyone in particular? Wire is having some official -- his word not mine -- documents drawn up so they'll have no choice but to hand her over," Boomer said.

"Send Patriot."

"You sure, Pres? He may scare the shit out of her."

"I'm sure." I leaned back in my chair. "He may be a big bastard, but he's got a gentle touch when it comes to wounded creatures."

"You're not wrong there. He's always mending some furball or another. All right. I'll send him just as soon as we have the papers from Wire." Boomer stepped out only to pause. "No one is getting your woman, Pres. We won't let them. Just sayin', we may want to bump up security. Doubt that grandfather of hers is the type to take no for an answer. He'll come for her, and he won't stop until he has her."

He wasn't telling me anything I didn't already know. Reinforcements were in order. I wasn't sure where we'd put everyone, but we'd figure it out. I dialed Spider, hoping he'd be willing to send a few brothers our way. If he didn't have anyone to spare, I'd hit some of the other clubs.

"Spider," the other Pres said as he answered.

"Need your help, brother. Got a situation that requires more men than I currently have available." I heard a squeal in the background and realized he was at home, probably spending time with his wife and daughter.

"How many you need?"

"Could you spare three?" I asked, knowing it was doubtful. Just depended on what the hell our Missouri chapter was facing right now.

"Not right now. I could send Cotton and maybe Hornet. You need more than that, I'd suggest you hit up the Devil's Boneyard. Things have been quiet over that way so I'm sure they could spare a few men," Spider said. "You know I'm not really handling this shit anymore, but I'll do what I can. Holding Church in a few days and I'm officially stepping down. You'll want to call Fox. I'm taking it to a vote, but I'm one hundred percent sure he'll be stepping up as Pres and Rocket will mostly likely be the new VP."

"Damn, brother. Lots of changes, but I get it. Appreciate the help. I'll call them next, and if you can spare both Cotton and Hornet, that would be great. I'll take anyone I can get."

"What the hell are you up against now?" Spider asked.

"Honestly? We found out MaryAnne is being abused, so I have to send someone to bring her here. Galahad and one of the prospects nearly died when a deal went sideways. They'll be out of commission for a while. Galahad needed surgery. I claimed a woman. Delilah. Her grandfather is bad news and I think he's coming for her. Need extra protection. Also have some other shit I need to handle in the upcoming week. I'm spread too thin."

"Sounds like you need an infusion of fresh blood," Spider said.

"Just patched in Galahad not too long ago. Riley and Morgan both have a year in now. Morgan is laid up at the moment. Could take it to a vote and see if we're going to patch them or let them go. The others are too new. Haven't proven themselves yet."

"How many Prospects will that leave you?"

"Three."

"You can do just fine with three. Not going to tell you how to run your chapter, but if it were me, I'd patch in those other two. Long as you can trust them to have your back."

"I trust them," I said. "Still doesn't give me enough manpower for right now. I'll call the Devil's Boneyard and start there. I won't take any chances with Delilah's safety."

"Good luck," Spider said, then hung up.

I scrolled through my contacts. I knew Cinder had stepped down as Pres, but I didn't have Charming's number in my phone. Instead, I called their VP, Scratch, and hoped he could help or at least give me the right number to call.

"Scratch," he said as he answered.

"It's Titan. I need some help. Wanted to call your Pres, but I don't have Charming's number. Still have Cinder in my phone."

Scratch grunted and I heard a chair creak. "What kind of help?"

I explained what had happened, what I thought was heading our way, and that I needed a few extra hands. After a bit more discussion, he agreed to speak with Charming but didn't see why they couldn't help me out. I hung up, hoping to hear back soon. Until I knew for certain if the Devil's Boneyard would send someone, I didn't want to call around to any other clubs.

I rubbed at my eyes, trying to wipe away the headache. I needed to wade through more paperwork, hear back from Scratch, and then I could head home and see my woman. I signed off on the account transfers Pretty Boy recommended, looked over a contract for a potential security job, then decided I was done for the day. My phone rang just as I stood.

"Titan," I said as I answered.

"It's Charming. Heard you need some help. Samurai is newly patched, but he's a good kid. I'm sending him and Rooster your way. Should be there later tonight."

"Appreciate it."

"I talked to the Dixie Reapers this morning. I know your woman is related to a man they'd like to put six feet under. I'll help in whatever way I can, not just to keep her safe, but to get rid of that asshole grandfather of hers."

"You ever need anything, give me a call," I said.

"Don't worry. I will." I could hear the smile in his voice, then the click as he hung up. Wasn't a sound you heard that often anymore, but some of the clubs did still have at least one landline.

I stretched, my back cracking and popping. I locked up my office and headed for my bike out front. It was time to head home. I was a little surprised I hadn't heard from Delilah all morning. Either she'd finally settled in a bit more, or she hadn't settled enough that she felt comfortable interrupting me. Now that she'd met Phoebe, I'd hoped the two of them would become friends.

I started up my bike and pulled away from the clubhouse. There was no greater feeling than the wind in my hair, except for perhaps the tight clasp of my woman's pussy. I grinned as I pulled into my driveway. Having Delilah in my bed was like having my own little porn star. Even though she wasn't doing the webcam stuff anymore, she was a little hellcat in bed. There were so many things I wanted to explore with her.

When I stepped into the house, the first thing I noticed was the quiet. No TV. No music. I wandered through the lower level, not finding Delilah anywhere, or Barney for that matter. The little furball hadn't even come to greet me. I climbed the stairs and went straight to our room, hoping that's where I'd find her. Barney lay outside the bathroom door, stretched along the doorway. His ear twitched but otherwise he ignored me. I stripped off my cut and set it on the dresser before going into the bathroom.

Delilah lay in the tub, her head tipped back, eyes closed. Her chest rose and fell steadily. I leaned against the doorframe and smiled. Prettiest picture I'd ever seen. Whatever she'd used to make the water bubble up had started to dissipate and only a slight foam remained along the surface. Not enough to hide her body from me.

Moving closer, I knelt next to the tub and ran my fingers down her arm. She moaned slightly and turned her face to the side. I hadn't noticed the dark smudges under her eyes before. Even though I kept her up most nights, I'd always let her sleep the next morning. I had to wonder if she was getting out of bed shortly after I left.

"Lilah," I said, rubbing her arm a little firmer. "Wake up, baby."

She murmured something and nearly slid down under the water. I caught her and held her up with one hand while I pulled the stopper on the tub with the other. The water gurgled as it went down the drain and still she didn't stir. I reached over for her towel, yanking it off the counter, then managed to wrap it around her upper body before I hauled her from the tub.

She cuddled against me as I carried her into the bedroom. I didn't give a shit if the sheets got a little wet. Easing her down onto the mattress, I gently dried her and tossed the towel aside. It only took a moment to strip out of my clothes. Crawling into the bed with her, I held her close and breathed in her scent.

Delilah clung to me. I ran my hand up and down her back, wondering how long she'd been sleeping in the tub. The water had been cold, and her skin held a chill. If she wasn't careful, she'd either get sick or end up drowning. I didn't want to think about her going under the water when I wasn't around to catch her. We hadn't been together very long, or known each other for an extended length of time, but I didn't like the thought of not having her in my life anymore.

"Justin?" she asked, her voice slurred from sleep.

"Right here, baby. You can sleep some more."

"So tired." I felt the sigh of her breath against me and heard her even breathing. I wasn't sure she'd even fully woken up for that little bit of talking.

If I hadn't left my phone in my pants pocket, I'd message Bones and ask him to come check her over. I hadn't heard of any illnesses going around other than the flu and she wasn't running a fever, but it wouldn't hurt to make sure she wasn't getting sick. I turned to my side and pulled her against my chest, kissing the top of her head.

"Rest, baby. I've got you."

Had I scared her too much when I'd told her about her grandfather? Was that why she was so tired? Could she not sleep if I wasn't here with her?

My phone rang but I refused to get up and answer it. I always put my club first. This one time I figured they could handle shit on their own, or wait until I was available. Delilah needed me. I'd be lying if I said I didn't like being in bed with her. Didn't matter it was the middle of the day.

The damn phone went off three more times before whoever it was got the hint and stopped calling. Delilah slept through it. My stomach growled and I knew I'd have to get up and eat at some point. Not knowing if she'd eaten anything, I didn't like the idea of her sleeping the day away and not getting the nourishment she needed. No matter how much I wanted her, I'd keep my hands to myself tonight. It was clear she needed to sleep more than she needed to be fucked.

When I couldn't handle the noise my stomach was making for another moment, I carefully got out of bed, pulling the covers over her. I yanked on my jeans, checked my phone, and went down to the kitchen with Barney on my heels. The missed calls were from a Prospect, which meant he'd probably called Boomer when he couldn't reach me. I decided to check in just the same, and make sure whatever it was had been handled. Right after I let Barney out. I had no idea when he'd last gone outside and I didn't want to add puddle cleanup to my to-do list for the day.

"What's going on, Shay?" I asked when he picked up.

"Had some folks at the gate. Said they were here to see your woman."

Every muscle in my body tensed. "Who were they?"

"Her parents, or so they said. Took a picture of their licenses and sent it over to Wizard. Haven't heard back yet. Thought you'd want to know about it, though."

"Thanks for calling. Boomer know what's going on?"

"Yeah, I told the VP," he said. "And Kraken."

"You did good, Shay. My woman is resting. She's looking a bit run-down. Can you send Bones this way? And if anyone needs me, make sure it's an emergency."

"You got it, Pres."

The line went dead, and I put my phone away. The clock on the stove said it was nearly two in the afternoon. I didn't see any dishes in the sink, so either Delilah hadn't eaten breakfast, or she'd cleaned up after herself. I'd noticed she tended to keep things tidy so it was possible the dishes had been washed.

A quick look in the fridge and cabinets was enough of a reminder we needed to hit the grocery store soon. I managed to find a package of pasta, a jar of sauce, and a pound of ground beef that hadn't expired just yet. It wasn't perfect, but it would be filling. I knew Delilah would season the meat if she made it, but aside from salt and pepper I didn't know a damn thing about seasoning shit. Phoebe had brought over a bunch of spices and such a while back, but I never used them. While the noodles cooked, I browned the meat and let the sauce warm on a back burner. One of the spice containers looked to be a blend of some sort. I sniffed it and decided it would work well enough with spaghetti, then sprinkled some over the meat while it cooked.

Barney barked and scratched at the back door, so I let him in. I got a treat down from the cabinet by the sink and gave it to him. He ran as fast as his short little legs would carry him and a moment later I heard him scrambling up the stairs.

I drained the noodles first so the grease from the meat wouldn't coat them. Delilah always ran hot water in the sink before she drained ground beef so I did the same. Probably explained why I needed to have the kitchen sink unclogged about two or three times a year. I'd never thought to run hot water before, during, and after to wash the grease all the way through the pipes.

I tossed the meat, sauce, and pasta together. After I pulled down two plates and glasses, got out some forks and shredded cheese, I left everything on the counter and went to check on Delilah. She still slept, which worried me. I sat on the edge of the bed and ran my fingers through her hair.

Barney nudged me with his cold nose, clearly worried about her too.

"Delilah, you need to get up. It's time to eat."

She murmured something I couldn't understand and cracked her eyes open. She blinked at me like a sleepy owl before yawning and struggling to sit up. I wrapped an arm around her waist and hauled her against my side.

"I don't know why I can't seem to wake up," she said.

"I found you asleep in the tub. I dried you off and put you to bed, but you've been asleep for at least a few hours, possibly longer since both you and the water were cold."

"I woke up sometime after you'd left and made it as far as the bathroom before I felt like I couldn't stay awake. I went back to sleep and when I got up again I decided to take a bath."

I held her tighter. "I'm going to have Bones take a look at you. He's the closest thing we have to a doctor, but if you'd prefer an appointment in town, I'll make it happen."

"Bones is fine," she mumbled.

I needed to tell her about her family showing up. I hadn't checked in with Wizard yet, or gotten any more calls, but if her parents had come by once, they'd keep coming until they got to see their daughter. I knew it's what I would do. Actually, I wouldn't have been sent away in the first place.

"Your parents are here. At least, a couple came to the gate saying they were your parents. I haven't checked with anyone yet to see if they really were. Would you like to have them over for a visit?" I asked.

She lifted her head, her eyes a little wider. "They're here? Just the two of them? Or did my brothers come too?"

"No one mentioned your brothers, so I assumed it was just your parents."

She patted the bed and looked around the room. "Where's my phone? I need to call Mom."

I reached over to the bedside table and picked her phone up, then handed it to her. She quickly located her mom under her contacts and put it on speaker.

"Delilah, are you okay?" her mom asked the second the call connected.

"I'm okay. I'm just really tired today for some reason."

I heard an indrawn breath. "They didn't drug you, did they?"

"I didn't drug your daughter," I said. "She's one of the most important people in my life. I'd never do anything to hurt her."

"You have me on speaker?" her mother asked in a tone only moms could manage.

Delilah cringed a little. "I don't keep things from Titan, Mom. And no, he didn't drug me. I'm probably coming down with something. That's not why I called. Are you in town?"

"Of course we are," her mom said.

"We?" Delilah asked. "As in you and Daddy?"

"Griffin came too," her mom said.

Delilah closed her eyes and shook her head. "I'm not two. I don't need babysitters. If you just came to visit, that's fine. I'd love to see you. If the three of you are checking up on me like I'm a runaway teen, then you shouldn't have bothered."

I heard the sound of the phone being passed to someone else.

"I know you're not a child, Delilah, but you'll always be my little girl. Is it wrong we want to make sure you're safe?" her father asked.

"No, Daddy. It's not. And if you want to come over, I only ask that you give me a little time to wake up good and get dressed. Like I told Mom, I'm really tired today and probably coming down with a bug."

"Are those assholes you're staying with going to let us in this time?" her dad asked.

"I'll make sure you're allowed in and escorted to my house," I said. "Your daughter lives here and you're welcome to visit. It's just better to give us a little notice next time."

"Thirty minutes. That's as much time as I can give her before her mother loses her shit. I think seeing your... whatever you call it, with all the fencing and guards, freaked her out."

"It's a compound," I said. "And it's meant to be intimidating."

Her dad hung up without another word and I felt Delilah sag against me. I had a feeling she wasn't up to this visit. Between her lack of excitement over seeing her family, and her fatigue, I was getting really worried about her. I hoped like hell Bones was on his way over. As much as I didn't want her leaving the safety of the compound, I'd take her to the doctor if I needed to. Delilah's safety didn't mean much if she was sick and needed medical attention.

"Come on, baby. You need to eat something. I made spaghetti, but it's probably gotten cold by now."

I helped her off the bed, pulled one of my shirts over her head, and led her downstairs. This time, Barney didn't follow. Delilah would need more clothes on before her family arrived, but right now I just wanted to get some food into her. The fact she'd slept all day meant she hadn't eaten since last night.

While she sat at the table, I reheated the pasta before I dished it out onto the plates and sprinkled cheese over it. I handed her a plate and got her a glass of sweet tea. By the time I sat down, she'd only managed a few bites. Her lack of enthusiasm over the food might have dented my ego if she didn't look so pale.

"Aren't you hungry?" I asked.

"I don't have much of an appetite right now," she said.

I pushed my plate away and stood. Walking to her side, I lifted her into my arms and carried her upstairs. Barney didn't budge and let out a little snore as I walked past him and into the bathroom. I stripped both of us and got into the shower with her. Delilah could barely stand on her own and seemed to be getting worse by the minute. After a shower didn't seem to invigorate her even a little, I helped her dry off and into some pajamas. It wasn't perfect, but other than Bones, the only people who would see her were her family.

I'd just helped her back into bed and pulled on my jeans when I heard a knock at the door. Barney started barking and raced down the stairs. Delilah moaned from the bed but didn't seem to be getting up.

I pressed a kiss to her brow and went down to get the door, hoping like hell it was Bones and not her family.

Seeing the club medic on my doorstep gave me a rush of relief. I almost yanked him into the house. "Delilah is in bed. She's been asleep all day, can hardly stand, doesn't have an appetite... I don't know what's wrong."

"Do I have permission to head up and check her over?" Bones asked.

"Wouldn't have asked you to come if I didn't want your help."

He slapped me on the shoulder and headed up the stairs. Since Delilah's parents were probably on their way, I locked the door. The last thing I wanted was them walking in unannounced. I took the stairs two at a time and hurried to the bedroom. Bones had already started examining Delilah, a frown marring his face. I heard him softly ask her questions, and she answered, but her words slurred a little.

"I think she has mono," Bones said.

Shit. "Where the fuck did she get it?"

"My best guess is her previous roommates. Both Missy and Rissa have it. Neither has been at the clubhouse for several days."

"I've never had it before. Does she need medication? Will I get it?" I asked.

"There's a chance you could get it. The best thing she can do is sleep. Her throat has started to hurt in addition to her other symptoms. Tylenol might make her feel better, and you need to keep her hydrated."

"Her parents are on their way over," I said.

"I'd keep them away if you can. I know they're probably worried about her, but she's not going to be up for company. You can let them see she's alive. Keep the visit short. She'll probably sleep through it."

"Thanks, brother. She scared the shit out of me when she wouldn't wake up."

"She probably contracted mono about four weeks ago. It has a four to six week incubation period. Poor girl is going to be miserable for a bit." Bones pulled the blanket up higher, covering Delilah all the way to her chin. "I'll see myself out."

I sat on the edge of the bed and watched her sleep. Her breathing was already deep and even, despite the fact she'd been talking to Bones a few moments ago. Whatever it took, I'd keep her safe, even against nasty illnesses. But first, I had to tell her family they needed to come back when she was feeling better. I had no doubt it wouldn't go over well.

Chapter Eight

Delilah

Three miserable weeks. Today was the first day I'd managed to get out of bed and not fall asleep on the couch within minutes. I felt like I'd been run over by a truck, then it backed up over me just to make sure I was dead. It didn't help my parents were here. Titan had convinced them to go home the day they'd arrived, but now that I was on the mend, they were back to see for themselves that I was still breathing. I didn't know why they thought Titan was going to hurt me. If anything, it seemed I had more to worry about from my own family. Which brought me to the extremely awkward conversation I needed to have with them.

"Mom, you said grandfather wanted you to marry someone else."

My mother nodded. "Thomas Kale III. I disliked the man, a lot. Meeting your dad was fate. He saw me, knew he wanted me, and decided to keep me. We were married less than two days after we'd met."

"What do you know about the agreement between your father and your intended?" Titan asked.

I reached over and took his hand. Thankfully, he hadn't gotten sick. Yet. I knew there was still a chance, but hopefully it passed him by. I'd never felt so horrible in my life.

"Just that it was some sort of business deal," my mom said, her brow furrowed. "Why? The way you asked, it sounds as if you suspect something else was going on."

Titan leaned back and studied my mom and dad a moment. Whatever he saw in my dad's eyes must have convinced him he could tell them the truth.

"Your father isn't a nice man," he said. "He brokers deals for rich, powerful men, to get the women they want. Some they marry, although the women are still little more than slaves. The rest don't even get the pretense of decency."

"Are you…" My mother clamped her lips tight.

"He's selling women?" my dad asked.

Titan nodded. "He is. We have proof, and so do the Dixie Reapers. They're hoping to take him down, and anyone else involved. In the meantime, I'm concerned for Delilah."

"What does that bastard want with my daughter?" my dad asked.

"One of the hackers got into your father-in-law's files. He has a contract for Delilah to marry one of his associates. The day he found out she'd moved here and was living with me, one of the Dixie Reapers observed him in an agitated state on his phone. We think it's possible he'll try to get his hands on her," Titan said.

"Over my dead fucking body," my dad said.

"Lance." Mom put her hand on his thigh. "I know you had your reservations about Delilah and Titan being together, but it's obvious she's safe here. This place is well-guarded, and you can tell this isn't just a fling for either of them. He cares about her."

My dad nodded. "You're right. I came here thinking she was being kept against her will. Now that I've seen them together, I know that isn't the case. I'm sorry I didn't wait until I had all the facts, but Delilah is my only little girl, and she's my youngest."

"I understand," Titan said.

I yawned and closed my eyes, leaning against Titan.

"Why don't I go upstairs with Delilah?" my mom offered. "She's still not quite back on her feet."

"I was going to make lunch," I murmured.

"You okay with pizza?" Titan asked. I wrinkled my nose and he laughed softly. "All right. No pizza. I'll get Chinese and order you some egg drop soup."

Mom took my arm and led me from the room, leaving Titan and my dad to talk. At least I didn't have to worry about them killing one another. If anything, my dad seemed to have grudgingly accepted Titan as my chosen guy. Although, it probably had more to do with the safety of the compound than anything else.

I pointed the way to our room and Mom helped me into bed, drawing the covers over me like she'd done when I was little. She brushed my hair back from my face and kissed my forehead. I heard the scrabble of paws and smiled, knowing Barney had followed.

"Is he allowed on the bed?" Mom asked. "Because I think he wants up here with you."

"Titan hasn't had him on the bed before, but I could use a good puppy cuddle right now."

My mom scooped up Barney and set him on the bed. He wriggled, his butt shaking so hard I worried he'd fall off the bed. Once he settled next to me, I wrapped my arm around him and almost immediately felt better.

"This dog doesn't exactly match your big, scary biker," Mom said.

"He saved Barney. Found him on the street, starved and covered in fleas."

"Guess it just goes to show you can't tell a good man just by outward appearances. Your grandfather is always well put together and charming. But he's selling girls. I can't even... How did I not know what a monster he was? And I let him get close to you and your brothers! What does that say about my parenting skills?"

"It says you have a good heart and wanted to forgive your dad," I told her. "I don't blame you, Mom. Or Dad. Neither of you could have known how bad he was. He was going to sell you, and me. What kind of man does that?"

"It was a common practice at one time. Signing contracts to combine lands, align empires, or secure the safety of future generations. But your grandfather? The only reason he has is pure greed and downright evilness lurking in his heart."

"I guess it's a good thing you only had one daughter. Then again, he may have friends who want men instead of women. I don't see Griffin being bullied into a marriage with someone, or just being given away and kept as a sex slave. He might be kind of pretty, but he's mean as a damn snake when you piss him off. He'd go after them like an enraged honey badger."

Mom snickered. "You're not wrong."

"How long do you think I'll have to stay locked behind the gates? I'm not exactly ready to venture out yet, especially since I'm still getting better, but I don't want to be stuck in the house indefinitely either."

"Once I was married to your dad and he'd taken my virginity, my father had to be more careful. He was angry, but he couldn't just grab me and run. I was an adult so he didn't have any control over me, other than money. Your dad would have never stopped looking if I'd gone missing, and I think my father realized that. I ruined his plans, and he wanted to ruin your dad in return."

"Why didn't you ever tell me all this?" I asked.

"I guess I wanted to protect you. He seemed different with you and the boys. I thought maybe he'd changed. It seems I was wrong."

"Does Griffin know? Or the others?" I asked.

"No. We never told them either. Now that your grandfather is showing his true colors again, we'll have to let them know what's going on. I don't want any of them accidentally giving him information on how to find you. He knows you moved away, and we mentioned you'd moved in with a biker, but I don't think we said the name of the town. I'm hoping it will take him a while to locate you. Long enough someone can put a stop to him and whoever he's working with."

I closed my eyes and wished this was all a nightmare. At least when I'd been too sick to stay awake for long, I hadn't worried about my grandfather. Or much of anything except no longer feeling so miserable. I still tired easily. From what Bones said, it would probably take another week or two before I felt completely normal again.

"You think Dad and Titan are getting along okay?" I asked.

"Now that your daddy knows that man only wants to keep you safe, you won't have any trouble out of him. He was ready to charge in here and save you. I can't even complain that he's quite a bit older than you since I'm younger than your daddy."

"I keep waiting for the day he decides being with me was a mistake. We've talked a little, and I've met his family, but we don't really have much in common. It's not just the age thing, although I'm sure that contributes to some of our differences."

Mom patted my hip through the blankets. "Honey, you don't want a man who loves everything you do. You've heard the saying opposites attract. That's what happened with you and Titan, and with me and your daddy. He'll like things, or do things that drive you crazy, but at the end of the day, those will also be the things that endear him to you. It's the differences that will keep things entertaining."

"If you say so," I mumbled.

"You have any other questions for me?" she asked.

"Like what?"

Mom squirmed a little. "Well… as far as I know, you hadn't had sex before you came here. I'm not stupid enough to think you're sharing this room with him and sex isn't part of it."

I couldn't contain my snort or the laughter that followed. "Mom, I'm not a virgin. I may have technically been one when I met Titan, but I took my own virginity a while ago. Between the books I read and the porn I've watched, I probably know more about sex than you do."

Her cheeks flushed and she sucked her lips into her mouth. "I wouldn't be too sure of that. Your daddy wasn't exactly a saint before he met me. Isn't one now either, for that matter."

I covered my ears and sang, "La-la-la-la. I can't hear you!"

Mom swatted me. "Oh, hush. Did you think the stork dropped you off?"

"Yep. That's exactly what I thought because the last thing I want to think about is you and daddy having sex. It was bad enough to see the two of you kissing all the time, or him smacking you on the ass whenever he'd walk by you. If I think about the stuff you two do behind a closed bedroom door, I'll be scarred for life and need lots of therapy."

Mom rolled her eyes. "So dramatic."

"Said the mother of four who just rolled her eyes like a teenage girl."

"I'm going to assume the sass is because you don't feel well." She eyed me with what I'm sure she thought was a look that would have me quaking in fear. Except my mom had never been able to pull off the "scary mom" vibe. Even when she'd gotten angry, none of us had been afraid of her.

"Love you, Mom," I said.

"I love you too, sweet girl."

I heard the heavy tread of steps on the stairs and a moment later Titan came into the room. "Food's here. You hungry?"

"Maybe a little," I said.

He came around the side of the bed and uncovered me, then picked me up and carried me downstairs. Mom trailed behind him. The smell of Chinese food hit me, and my stomach rumbled. I couldn't remember the last time I'd eaten much of anything. I felt weak as a newborn kitten. Titan eased me down onto a kitchen chair. There was a plastic container of egg drop soup in front of me, and a spoon.

"Also got you some fried rice. Just don't eat too much of it until you know it's going to hit your stomach okay," he said, sliding a carton toward me. "It's chicken. I know you like the shrimp better, but seafood after being sick didn't seem like a great idea."

He wasn't wrong about that. Just the thought of shrimp made me feel a little green. Mom opened a carton of orange chicken and I covered my mouth. I stood quickly, nearly hitting the floor as my legs gave out. Titan wrapped an arm around my waist and carried me over to the kitchen sink.

"I'm not puking in the sink," I said through the fingers covering my mouth.

He quickly grabbed the kitchen trash can and brought it over. The second the smell hit me, I threw up. I heard the scrape of a chair and knew my dad had beat a hasty retreat. If he heard someone throwing up, then he usually joined them. Titan held my hair until I had nothing left in my stomach. I leaned over the sink and rinsed my mouth before splashing cool water on my face.

My mother came to stand next to me, leaning against the counter. She eyed Titan, then me before turning her gaze back to him. "Any chance you knocked her up?"

It felt like the world was spinning. "I'm on birth control."

"Been taking it regular? Pills? Shots? What are you on?" Mom asked.

"The pill. I've been on it about a month and a half, and I've mostly been taking them. I missed a few."

My mother muttered something I didn't quite catch. "Delilah, you can't miss doses. But let's forget that for a moment. How long were you taking them before you started seeing Titan? Or more accurately, before you started sleeping with him, and did the two of you ever use any other protection?"

"We didn't," he answered.

"I was on them about two weeks. Why?" I asked.

"Because, my precious, clueless baby girl, you didn't listen to a damn thing the doctor said when you got on them. If you had, you'd know you have to take them a month before they're effective, and you can't miss any," Mom said.

I was scared to look at Titan. Was he mad? Or did he feel anything at all about it? My stomach gurgled and flipped. For that matter, how did I feel about it? I wanted to be a mom -- someday -- but I'd wanted to wait a little longer. Maybe she was wrong. Maybe it was just the mono and my weakened body.

Titan pressed a kiss to the top of my head. I looked up and saw him put his phone to his ear.

"Bones, I need a pregnancy test for Delilah," he said. "I don't care what kind or how many, but I want it done within the hour."

The club medic must have agreed because Titan hung up.

"Are you mad?" I asked. "I swear I didn't know. If they said anything when I got the prescription, I didn't remember."

"Not mad, baby. Let's find out for sure if you're pregnant and we'll go from there."

"I'll just go check on your dad," Mom said. "Let him know it's safe to come back in."

Titan pulled me against him, holding me tight. I breathed him in and wrapped my arms around his waist. His heartbeat was slow and steady against my cheek. At least he wasn't freaking out over this. Or if he was, he'd mastered the art of remaining physically calm.

My mom and dad came back into the room and reclaimed their seats at the table.

"We'll go back to the hotel soon," Mom said. "But if you might be pregnant, we'd like to be here when you find out. If that's all right with the two of you?"

"It's fine with me," Titan said.

"Never thought Delilah would be the first to make us grandparents," my dad said. "Figured it would be Ben."

"That's because our middle son takes after his daddy," Mom said with a smirk.

"Um, I love you both, but I think this conversation is going somewhere uncomfortable," I said.

"She thinks the stork dropped her off," Mom said.

I heard the front door open and Bones yelled out, "Where is everyone?"

"Kitchen," Titan called back.

The club medic walked in, paused to check out my mom -- until my dad glared at him, then he brought over a plastic sack and handed it to me. "Three different tests."

I took the bag, my cheeks warming at the thought of everyone knowing I was about to go pee on these stupid things. I pulled away from Titan and went to the downstairs bathroom. After I shut the door, I pulled out the three tests and set them on the counter. Even though I knew the basics of how it worked, I read the instructions for each. I locked the door, then took each test, putting them back on the bathroom counter when I was done.

Three minutes. It didn't seem like a long time, except when you were waiting on a life-changing event. The seconds moved so slowly I nearly started chewing on my nails. I didn't have a clock handy, but I kept eying the sticks. When the first one showed a positive sign, I almost dropped to the floor. Pregnant? I waited on the other two, thinking maybe the first one was a false positive. I'd heard it happened, especially with the tests you bought at the store.

Nope. All three said the same thing. There was a life growing inside me.

"Delilah." Titan's voice was soft on the other side of the door. "You okay, baby?"

"I-I'm not sure."

The doorknob rattled and I remembered I'd locked it. I twisted the lock and he opened the door, took one look at my face, then moved over to the counter and stared at the sticks. I wasn't sure what to expect from him. It definitely wasn't the slow smile that spread across his lips, or the excitement in his eyes.

"We're having a baby." He pulled me against him and kissed the hell out of me. "You've made me so fucking happy, Lilah."

"You're okay with me being pregnant? It's so soon, and you'd wanted to wait before starting a family."

"Baby, I have a family, but I missed out on so much with Phoebe. I didn't know about her until she'd already had a kid and married Kraken." He kissed me again. "This time, I get to be there from the beginning."

Well, at least he wasn't pissed.

"Guess we better tell my parents the news," I said.

"Oh, hell no. Baby, that's all you."

I patted his chest. My big, bad biker. Afraid of telling my parents he'd knocked me up. It was kind of cute.

Chapter Nine

Titan

Gwen and Lance had decided to stick around a few days, so I'd left Delilah in their capable hands while I took care of club business. Mostly, they'd stayed at my house while she regained her strength. Until this morning when Gwen had mentioned baby shopping. I'd made it clear Delilah wasn't to leave the compound, which had only made Gwen roll her eyes and show me the various shopping apps on her phone. I'd handed over my credit card, given them a limit, and briskly walked out of the house. Lance had given me a knowing smirk, and I'd barely resisted from flipping him off. Figured it wasn't wise to piss off my woman's dad.

I pulled up at the clubhouse and shut off my bike right as Patriot came through the gate in his old Bronco. The fact he was shirtless wouldn't have made me hesitate if it weren't for the woman sitting next to him in a tee that was clearly way too big on her small frame. He stopped a few feet away and I walked over to his window. The woman cast me furtive glances and looked about two seconds from jumping out of her skin. MaryAnne Swenson. Whatever Wire had done, it seemed to have worked. Unless Patriot destroyed the building and everyone in it when he went to get her.

He rolled down the window and positioned his body to block her from my view. Or more likely to block me from hers.

"Taking her to my place for now," Patriot said. "She needs to get cleaned up, have a decent meal, and she's going to need clothes."

"I'll see if Phoebe has anything she can borrow. Might not be a perfect fit, but it's better than nothing.

Once you figure out her sizes, I'll set aside some money from club funds to buy what she needs. You can either shop online, or take her to the store if she's up for it." I dropped my voice lower. "She know about Galahad?"

"Told her Sean patched in, but we haven't discussed anything else," Patriot said.

"Get her home and taken care of. We can figure out something more permanent later. Thanks for handling this."

I smacked my hand against the door panel and went into the clubhouse. I didn't know where we'd put MaryAnne long-term, but for now she seemed okay with Patriot. I knew he'd protect her, and she wasn't afraid of him. After all she'd suffered, there was no way she'd trust just anyone. Patriot must have done something to prove he wouldn't hurt her. Made me wonder exactly what went down when he picked her up, but I'd have to find out later.

Stone was at the bar sipping a beer. I claimed the stool next to him, hoping he'd heard something about the women we'd lost, and the fuckers who'd nearly killed Galahad and Morgan.

"The club's contact is dead," Stone said.

"Any idea what the fuck happened that day?"

"Show of power. They pocketed the cash, but didn't like the fact we were setting those women free. Decided to prove a point."

"Well, we can't let that fucking stand."

Stone took another swallow of his beer. "Figured you'd say that. Seeing as how you're going to be a daddy, and Kraken has two kids now, I think you should take a backseat on this one. I'll get it handled. Fuckers won't know what hit them."

"I trust you."

"Did you hear the Missouri chapter has a new Pres and VP?" he asked.

"Spider mentioned it when I spoke to him last. Said there would be a vote, but he figured Fox would be the new Pres and Rocket would be the VP. Not a bad idea to put some of the younger guys in the officer positions."

"We still keeping the others around? The help Spider and Charming sent?"

"Yeah. I know we haven't had much use for them yet, but until Delilah's grandfather is either dead or behind bars, I want the extra guns."

"They've set up a rotation between them for patrolling the compound. Partially boredom, I'm sure, but they also don't want anything to happen to your woman," Stone said.

"Make sure they have what they need. Anything need my immediate attention?"

"Other than your woman?" he asked.

"Fuck off. Delilah is fine. Her parents are with her."

"Met the brothers yet?"

"No. Thanksgiving isn't too far off. I'm sure Delilah will either want to go home, or ask them to come here. I'd hate to not be here with Phoebe and the kids. Not sure they'd be welcome to go with us."

Stone shrugged a shoulder. "So have her family come here. We can make sure we've got room for them. Besides, they're your family now too. You inherited them when you claimed Delilah."

He wasn't saying anything I didn't already know. So far, Gwen and Lance weren't so bad. The brothers, though, I had a feeling would be a problem. Delilah had said they were overprotective. If I'd had a little sister, I'd have been the same way. But if they tried to get between me and my woman, I'd put them in their place without hesitation. Didn't matter if anyone liked it or not. Delilah was mine. My woman. My...

Shit.

"I need to make a quick run somewhere. Hold things down here for me?"

"You got it, brother." Stone gave me a knowing look. "You making an honest woman of her?"

"Yeah, I think I am."

"Could just ask Wizard to handle it. No need for a preacher."

I stood and slapped him on the back. "Ask him to do it. In the meantime, I need a ring."

I went out to my bike and headed for town. I knew Kraken had given Phoebe a ring, but I wasn't sure where he'd purchased it. After driving around a bit, I found a jewelry shop and parked out front. The glittering display cases, and the suit-wearing man behind the counter, made me think I'd be spending a small fortune on anything I bought there. As long as it was quality, I didn't care about much else.

I'd given one of my cards to Delilah, but I had another I seldom used for anything. If this place didn't have a ring that wouldn't put me over the credit limit, I'd find another. I walked inside and the man immediately sneered as he took in my cut and boots. Yeah, I didn't exactly blend in a place like this. Didn't mean my money didn't spend just as well as anyone else's.

"Need a ring," I said.

The man gave a delicate sniff and pointed to a glass case on the far wall. "Anything in your budget will be over there."

In my budget? I narrowed my eyes at him before checking out the rings he'd pointed out. They were each small, the diamonds so tiny I almost needed a magnifying glass to see them. Delilah deserved better than this. I moved along to another and another until I saw something I liked.

"How much is that one?" I asked, making sure I left a smudge on his pristine glass case.

He stared down his nose at me before checking the ring. "I'm sure it's out of your price range. Perhaps you'd do better shopping somewhere else."

Oh now the little fucker was just pissing me off. If I didn't know a place like this had a security button behind the counter, and cameras in the room, I'd pull my gun. I had no doubt a pansy like this one would shit his pants. Instead, I leaned a little closer and dropped my voice in a way I'd been told scared lesser men.

"Look here, you little pissant. I'm here to buy a ring for my woman and I'm not leaving without one. You either tell me how much that ring is, or I'll break this fucking case and check the tag myself."

He audibly swallowed and his hand shook as he unlocked the cabinet and pulled out the ring. He eyed the tag before giving me another snooty look.

"It's a one-carat diamond in a vintage rose gold setting, and the price is four-thousand two-hundred ninety-nine dollars." The man's fingers turned white, he was holding the ring so tightly.

I pulled out my wallet, making him flinch as I yanked it from my pocket. I tried not to laugh at his reaction. What a pussy. Whoever he was with must wear the pants in their relationship. I tossed my credit card onto the counter.

"I'm assuming you take credit cards."

The man grabbed the card and sprinted for the register, the ring still clutched in his hand. After the charge went through and he brought me the slip to sign, I made him clean the ring until it shone. Last thing I wanted was his fingerprints on it when I gave it to Delilah. He handed me my card back, along with the small black velvet box. I put my card in my wallet and tucked the ring into my front pocket.

I wanted tonight to be special. I didn't want to just hand Delilah the ring and tell her we were married. With her family visiting, I wasn't sure if I'd have a chance to get her alone until after dinner. Not unless I told her mom or dad what I'd planned.

I didn't like the idea of them knowing before her.

Looked like I'd be figuring this shit out after I got home.

When I pulled through the gate at the compound, Hornet flagged me down. I coasted closer to him and stopped the bike.

"Everything okay?" I asked.

"Been quiet here, Titan. You sure you need us? Spider and Fox asked us to stay as long as we were needed, but I don't think anyone's coming for your woman."

As much as I wanted to send him back to the Missouri chapter, something told me things were far from over with Gregory Montcliff. Man like that didn't give up easy. He'd lost his daughter. No way he'd let Delilah slip through his fingers too. Not without making a fuss. The fact he'd been quiet so far, told me he was either gathering intel, wasn't entirely certain where Delilah was, or he'd already made a plan and was just biding his time. Whatever the case, I wanted to be ready when the snake struck.

"Hornet, I appreciate you being here, and I know you want to go home. If you could stay until I know for sure Gregory Montcliff, and his associates, won't be an issue for Delilah, I'd be grateful. You're my brother, and I'll have your back whenever you need me. I'm hoping you'll do the same."

He sighed and ran a hand through his hair. "Yeah, all right. I'll stay. Want me to tell the others? The Boneyard men are rumbling about there not being much to do, so it's not just me wondering."

"Tell you what. How about a party tonight? I'll make a call and get some extra girls at the clubhouse later. Just try to keep my in-laws out of there, and make sure any nudity remains inside the clubhouse and not out here. That's not something I want to explain to Gwen and Lance."

"Thanks, Titan. I'll spread the word."

I pulled away and went straight home. Before I went into the house, I sent a message to Missy. *Send some of your girls to the clubhouse if they want to party. Just no one who's been exposed to mono.*

She sent a thumbs-up emoji back, which was probably as good an answer as I was going to get. I was still pissed at her for letting Shella be a webcam girl, and for getting Delilah sick, but for all her faults, she always knew the right girls to send to the clubhouse to guarantee my brothers would have a good time. Those women were wild, and exactly what the single men needed right now.

I went inside and found Lance watching ESPN on the living room TV. He saluted me with a beer, but never looked away from the screen. I heard a giggle in the kitchen and found my woman and her mom at the table, a tablet sitting between them with a kitten video playing.

"Look, Titan! He's so cute!" Delilah said, pointing to the screen.

I peered down at the tablet and smiled as a fuzzy gray kitten chased after a ball, then slid across the floor and bounced off the wall. It shook its head before scampering off again.

"No kittens, Lilah. We already have Barney. He'll be jealous enough over a baby." I kissed the top of her head.

"All right." She fake pouted, her lower lip sticking out way too far. "But it's cute, isn't it?"

"Yes, it's cute. No, we don't need one."

Gwen snickered. "Good luck. You'll need it. First time you turn your back, she'll sneak one into the house and see how long it takes you to notice. She did that with a hamster, then had to confess what she'd done when it burrowed into the couch."

"Into the…" I shook my head. "I'm not sure I want to know how that turned out."

"No, you really don't," Lance said, coming into the room.

"Like I was the worst child ever?" Delilah asked. "Have you forgotten the stunts my brothers pulled? At least I didn't sneak a boy into the house."

Gwen groaned and laid her head on the table. "Griffin. That boy!"

Lance smirked. "I was both pissed and proud."

I lifted my eyebrows in a silent question.

"He snuck in a little cheerleader after everyone had gone to bed. We may not have noticed if they hadn't decided to have sex. Let's just say the girl had a set of lungs on her. The way she was carrying on, I was impressed," Lance said.

Gwen glowered at him. "You would be."

"I also grounded him because girls weren't allowed in his room with the door closed, much less when no one else was awake. Although we certainly didn't stay asleep for long with all that racket going on."

"Makes your daughter downright angelic," I said.

"Now *that* I don't need to hear," Lance said.

Delilah rolled her eyes, but I saw the slight smile on her lips. "I think he's just trying to say that he was my first and only, Daddy. I didn't sneak boys in at home because I'd never been with anyone until Titan."

"So you took her innocence and you knocked her up." Lance shook his head. "Guess you don't do anything halfway."

And there was my opening. This wasn't the romantic setting I'd wanted for Delilah, but it would have to do.

"About that. Wizard is a hacker, and he's helped with some legal issues here and there. Thing is, he decided to dip into the county and state records. As of today, we're married," I said, as I pulled the ring from my pocket. "I know it's not the wedding you probably dreamed of, but it will look completely legal to anyone who goes digging for a marriage certificate."

I took the ring from the box and slid it onto her finger. It was a little loose, but I knew she could get it sized later. Delilah looked up at me with tears in her eyes.

"I fucked this up, didn't I?" I asked.

She shook her head. "It's perfect. I love the ring, and I don't need a church wedding or anything. I didn't think I even needed to be married to you at all, until you said I was now your wife."

"On that note, maybe we should leave and give you two some space," Gwen said, standing from the table.

"Stay," I said. "If you don't mind, I'd like to invite my daughter and her family over."

Gwen's mouth opened and shut a few times. She shared a look with Lance, and I realized they either didn't know about Phoebe or hadn't understood she was old enough to have kids of her own.

"You'll like her, Mom," Delilah said.

"You knew he had a daughter old enough to have her own family?" Gwen asked.

Delilah nodded. "Yes. I've met them. His grandkids are really cute."

"Your grandkids now," Lance muttered. "Jesus."

"I'll place an order with the Italian place in town, if you're up for lasagna?" I asked Delilah, not sure what she could or couldn't handle right now. "Kraken can pick it up or ask a Prospect to go get it. That way you don't have to worry about making dinner."

"Sounds good," Delilah said. "Maybe banana pudding for dessert? Do they have any?"

"If not, I'll find some." I leaned down to kiss her softly. "Anything else you want?"

She shook her head.

"I'll call Kraken and make sure they don't have plans. Either way, we can still have Italian and banana pudding." If my pregnant wife wanted a certain meal, I'd make damn sure she got it, even if it meant driving two towns away to find it. Granted, as the President, I didn't have to go get the items myself. Didn't mean I wouldn't.

I stepped out of the room to call Kraken before placing the order. If they were coming over, I'd order extra. If it would just be me, Delilah, and her parents, then I wouldn't need quite so much food. Although leftovers were never a bad thing.

The phone rang a few times before he picked up, sounding out of breath.

"Do I even want to know what you're doing?" I asked.

"Chasing Ember," he said. "She likes to play tag, except I'm always it."

I chuckled, knowing exactly what he meant. She'd giggle and squeal whenever someone chased after her, then when you caught her, she'd take off and want you to do it again. I loved that little girl more than I ever thought possible.

"Want to take a break and bring the family over? Delilah's parents are here. Thought y'all should meet, seeing as I'm married to her now."

It was quiet a moment. "Married?"

"Yep. Wizard handled it. Maybe not the most romantic way to do things, but Delilah didn't seem to care. Think her parents are a little surprised. Lance looked a bit relieved, though. Although, he appeared to like the idea of his little girl being married and not just shacking up."

"Can you blame him?"

No, I couldn't. Although, with the way Kraken treated Phoebe, and knowing he'd made her his old lady, I wouldn't have cared either way. I knew she was in good hands, but I also understood this lifestyle. For me, her being his old lady was enough. Lance and Gwen, from what I could tell and what Wizard had found, hadn't been exposed to club life. They'd done a few towing jobs for the Dixie Reapers, but never hung out with them.

"Y'all coming or not?" I asked.

"We'll be there. Just give your daughter time to pull herself together. If she's meeting new people, you know she'll want to look her best. Seeing as how Banner threw up on her, I'm thinking that means she'll want a shower."

"I'm going to place the order and have a Prospect pick it up. Get here whenever you can. Can't promise we'll wait to eat if you aren't here before the food, but we'll have plenty."

"Let me round them up. See you in a bit."

The line went dead. I pulled up the contact for the Italian place but paused as I heard a throat clear. I glanced over my shoulder at Lance.

"It seems our oldest has decided to come check out the place where his sister is living. We didn't know he was coming, but he's at the gate and said they won't let him in." Lance stared me down. "You going to let him in?"

"Depends. Is he going to be civil to Delilah and mind his manners?"

Lance's lips twitched as if he fought not to smile. "Probably not. You know how siblings are. Fight like cats and dogs, but when it comes down to it, he'd protect her against someone else. Might give you shit since you're older than her."

I gave a nod, appreciating his honesty, then sent a text to Shay. *Guy at the gate is Delilah's brother. Let him in and escort him to my house.*

I saw the little dots as he typed his response. *On it.*

"It's done. He'll be brought here in a few minutes. Guess I better expand the dinner order a little."

Lance pulled out his wallet and I waved him off. "No need. I've got it."

"All right. Well, if you change your mind, let me know. And you might want to triple the banana pudding order. Or quadruple it. Griffin can put away just as much if not more than Delilah. It's their favorite."

Good to know. I dialed the restaurant and placed the order, thankful they did in fact have the dessert my woman wanted. After I paid over the phone, I asked Owen to go pick it up and bring it by the house. There was a knock at the door, and I went to answer, figuring it was Shay and Delilah's brother.

The Prospect stood on the front step with a tall boy behind him. I knew the kid was older than Delilah, but he still had a baby smooth face and an innocence in his eyes. I motioned him in. Shay stepped inside first and lingered by the door, probably ready to make a break for it at any second. It wasn't the norm for me to have so many people stopping by my place if they weren't part of the club.

"Need anything else, Pres?" Shay asked.

"I think we're good. Thanks for bringing him, Shay."

He nodded and took off, almost running to his bike. I shut the door and focused on the kid. Griffin. He eyed me from the tips of my boots to the top of my head, not looking the least bit impressed. As his gaze skimmed the patches on my cut, there was a flicker in his eyes. Fear.

Wasn't anything I hadn't experienced before. Men saw a biker and automatically thought the worst. No, I didn't always walk on the right side of the law, but I didn't hurt the innocent either. When he was finished sizing me up, I waited for whatever would come out of his mouth.

"Did you take advantage of my sister?" he asked.

"She's my wife. That answer your question?"

"Not really. You're kinda old for her, don't you think?"

I took a step closer, then another. He backed up and I didn't stop until he'd hit the wall and had nowhere else to go. I used my height to my advantage, topping him by several inches.

"Look here, boy. That woman means everything to me. She's mine, and she's carrying my kid. If you came to cause trouble or stress her out, you can turn your ass around and leave right the fuck now."

Griffin audibly swallowed and gave a jerky nod. "Got it."

"She's in the kitchen with your parents."

I backed up and he almost sagged in relief. With one last glance at me, he hurried away and found his family sitting around the kitchen table. Lance looked from Griffin to me, then back again.

"You didn't try to measure dicks, did you?" Lance asked. "I'm betting his is bigger."

"Daddy!" Delilah shrieked.

Lance smirked and Gwen looked slightly amused. Griffin took a seat next to his mom and kept his mouth shut. Looked like I'd made an impression. Good. Last thing I wanted was him upsetting my woman.

"Dinner will be here before long, and Kraken is bringing Phoebe and the kids over. We'll have a full house." I stood behind Delilah and placed my hand on her shoulder, leaning down so only she could hear me. Or that had been my intention. "You get tired, it's okay to go lie down. No one expects you to entertain them."

The wink Gwen gave me was enough to know she'd heard me and approved.

"I'm fine, Titan," Delilah said, placing her hand over mine. "But I promise if it gets to be too much, I'll go to bed."

"Does everyone call you that?" Griffin asked. "Your wife doesn't even get to use a normal name for you? Or did your mom actually give you that name?"

"Griffin." Lance glared at his son. "You're in Titan's house, inside his compound. You know better than to disrespect someone when you're on their turf. Not to mention, he's family now. Watch your fucking mouth."

"I earned the name Titan, so yes, everyone uses it. To answer your other question, Delilah uses my given name when it's just the two of us. Calling me Titan when others are around is a sign of respect. And no, I'm not telling you my real name. You haven't earned the right to know it." I arched my eyebrows, daring him to say anything.

"Why are more people coming over?" he asked, directing his question to his dad.

"Because Titan has a daughter. Her family is coming over to meet us," Lance said.

I could tell Griffin wanted to say something about me having a fully grown daughter, but he refrained. Good thing too. I was about done with his shit. Even though I didn't know his exact age, he was damn sure old enough to know better than to mouth off to his sister's husband. Seeing my cut had gotten a reaction out of him. One I wanted to explore a little more, but not with an audience.

Hoped like hell he didn't say anything to piss off Phoebe, or worse, Kraken. There'd be no saving him then.

I might be protective of my daughter, but Kraken would destroy anyone who hurt Phoebe, even if it wasn't physical pain.

Chapter Ten

Delilah

I loved my brother. I really did. I wondered if I said that enough times in my head that I'd remember it and not want to throttle him. He'd been rude, not just to Titan, but to everyone. I didn't know how my big, scary biker hadn't stomped him into the ground yet. My dad had tried to reel him in, but once Griffin got going, there was no stopping him. Not nicely at any rate.

"Back the fuck off!" I yelled at him.

Griffin snapped his mouth shut and glared at me. "I'm trying to protect you! It's obvious letting you move away was a mistake. You don't make good decisions, Delilah. Look at you. You hooked up with the first biker who came along? What the hell else have you been doing?"

My back straightened and I walked closer to Griffin. Bringing my arm back, I let my hand fly and cracked him across the cheek with my palm. "How dare you! After everything you've done in the past, you dare to judge me?"

"Never thought my sister would be a whore," Griffin said.

The silence in the room was deafening. I felt the blood drain from my face as I stumbled out of the kitchen. We'd gathered in there to fix our plates, but I couldn't be near him right now. My hands were shaking, and it felt like I would fall apart at any moment. The room behind me exploded with angry shouts and tears pricked my eyes.

Did he really think that of me? He hadn't even known I was a webcam girl. If he did, it would only confirm his belief that I'd been whoring myself out. I heard a crash that sounded like a chair splintering, and Ember started to cry. Phoebe rushed out of the room with both kids, her eyes wide.

"I'm so sorry," I said.

"What the hell was that about?" Phoebe asked.

"I don't know." I sighed and rubbed at the headache building between my eyes. "My brothers have always been overprotective, which is why I moved away. I couldn't have a boyfriend because they always ran them off. But he's never acted like that, and he's certainly never called me a whore."

"I think I need to take the kids home. I don't want to risk them getting hurt now that the punches have started flying."

I winced. They were beating each other now? I moved past Phoebe and went into the kitchen. My dad was holding Griffin back as my brother struggled to get to Titan. My husband's lip was split and bleeding and his knuckles were bruised. I went to him, placing my hand on his arm, but he shook me off.

"Not now, Delilah." His voice was so... cold. I glanced at my dad and saw disappointment in his eyes. Even Kraken didn't seem all that happy with me. I hadn't done anything!

"Kraken, Phoebe wants to take the kids home."

"Can you blame her?" he asked, stomping past me.

My vision blurred as more tears gathered in my eyes. My mother wouldn't even look at me, and I wondered what had been said after I'd left the room. Griffin was the one being unreasonable!

"Why is everyone mad at me?" I asked.

"Delilah! I said not now," Titan said.

I sucked in a breath, looked at each of them, then walked out. Except I didn't stop in the living room. I needed air. Space. I felt like I was suffocating and the world was closing in on me. I made it to the front steps and sucked in cool air, hoping it would settle my nerves. Another crash sounded inside, and I heard someone shout my name.

I needed… needed… I glanced around and saw Griffin's truck. I knew he'd have left the keys under the visor since the vehicle was inside a locked compound, so I ran to it and jumped inside, not caring I was barefoot and didn't have my purse. I just had to get away even if for a few minutes so I could think and calm down.

I snatched the keys from their hiding place and started up the truck. As I pulled away from the house, not a single person ran out to stop me. I hoped they just hadn't realized I'd left. The thought of all of them letting me leave without even trying to stop me made my heart hurt.

I approached the gates of the compound and was thankful that it was dark outside, and for Griffin's tinted windows. The Prospect couldn't see me or he may have tried to stop me. I pulled through and turned right out of the compound, heading for the highway. Even though I didn't have a destination in mind, I'd always liked driving on the open road far more than riding around town.

As the truck ate up the miles, the town grew smaller in the rearview mirror until I couldn't see the lights at all. What I did see was one lone headlight, which meant I had a motorcycle behind me. I didn't remember anyone pulling out behind me at the compound. Of course, there were plenty of men who had motorcycles. Just because one was behind me didn't mean they were part of Hades Abyss.

My bladder started to scream at me, and I pulled off at the next exit. I stopped at a gas station and looked around the cab of Griffin's truck, hoping he had a pair of flip-flops or something in here I could use. Not only would they not let me into the store without shoes, I really, really didn't want to walk across the parking lot, much less into the bathroom, without something covering my feet.

A tap on the window made me scream and jolt in my seat. I looked over and saw a man in a leather cut standing next to the truck. I rolled the window partway down and saw his patches said *Devil's Boneyard MC* and his name was *Samurai*. I could understand where his name had come from. He didn't look a lot older than me, but it was clear he was at least half-Japanese.

"Titan is going to be pissed when he finds out you ran," Samurai said. "Where are you going?"

"You know Titan?"

He nodded. "I was sent from my club to help keep an eye on things until the danger is over. And here you are, out running around with no guard, just begging to get snatched. What were you thinking?"

"I just needed to get away, even for a little bit to clear my head. Everyone is screaming and fighting. My brother is calling me names. My parents are disappointed in me."

"Why are you stopping here?" he asked.

"I have to pee." My cheeks flushed. "But I don't have shoes. This is my brother's truck but he doesn't have anything I can wear inside and use the bathroom. Wait. How did you even know I was in this truck? The windows are so dark there's no way you saw me."

"Watched you get in. I'd been patrolling the back half of the compound and needed a beer. On my way to the clubhouse, saw you jump in and take off. Decided I'd better follow." He glanced at the store. "Wait here. I'll see if there's anything inside."

Before I could protest, he took off into the store. When he came back out a few minutes later, he had the ugliest pair of unicorn house shoes I'd ever seen. They had stuffed heads on top with rainbow manes sticking out in different directions. And they were neon pink. I eyed them, wondering if this was a joke.

"Sorry, darlin'. All they have are novelty items inside. These were the least offensive, if that tells you anything."

He handed them over and I slipped them onto my feet. I rolled up the window and shut off the truck, taking the keys with me as I stepped out onto the concrete. Samurai took my arm and led me inside. As I ducked into the bathroom, he waited outside the door, standing sentry to keep me safe. He seemed sweet and I wondered if he had a woman at home waiting for him. Guys like him didn't seem to exist anymore. Or so I'd thought.

I finished up, washed my hands, and went out into the store, suddenly so thirsty it felt like I'd swallowed an entire desert. As much as I wanted a bottle of water, I didn't have so much as a penny on me. Samurai noticed the direction of my gaze and led me over to the refrigerated cases.

"Get whatever you want," he said.

"You've spent enough on me already."

"And Titan will have my ass if you get dehydrated before I can get you safely back home. Now get something to drink. It's no more than a few dollars, Delilah. It's not going to bankrupt me."

I picked out an ice-cold bottle of water and let him pay at the counter. I'd guzzled half of it before I even made it back to the truck. Samurai helped me into the driver's seat and made sure I'd buckled before he shut the door. I locked it and waited for him to get on his bike. A black limo pulled into the lot, which struck me as odd for a rural area. I wondered if some teens had rented one for a special occasion, or maybe someone was celebrating.

I fiddled with the radio until I heard two shots. I jerked my head toward the window and saw Samurai on the ground, red spreading out around him. My brain didn't want to process what it meant. I kept watching and waiting. He didn't get up. My heart hammered in my chest and I fumbled with my seatbelt and the lock on the door. I nearly fell out of the truck as I hurried to his side.

His eyes were opened, his breathing labored. "Run."

I barely heard him, but the word was enough to make fear spike through me. *Run?* I looked around and saw two large men heading for me out of the shadows. I took off toward the truck. Just as my fingers brushed the door, one of them grabbed my hair and yanked me off my feet.

"Not so fast, little bitch. The boss has plans for you."

I fell to the ground, the concrete bruising my knees. I wrapped an arm around my stomach, trying to protect my baby. Whatever these men had planned for me, it couldn't be good. They didn't seem to care if they hurt me. And they'd shot Samurai! I glanced his way, hoping he was okay. His eyes had slid shut and he looked far too pale. I saw the clerk in the store on the phone. Maybe an ambulance would arrive in time to save him.

I heard sirens in the distance, and so did the men. One hauled me up, holding my arm with a tight grip. He dragged me to the limo and shoved me into the backseat before following me in. Did these idiots not realize a car like this would stick out in a small town? I only hoped it made the car easier to track. Another man was already inside. He started wrapping a rope around my wrists, and another around my ankles.

"Be a good girl and you'll be okay," he said. "Boss needs you in good shape for what he has planned."

My stomach soured. That didn't sound remotely good.

"Wait. I... I'll go with you and I won't fight, just... Could you please get Samurai some help? He was only protecting me."

"Fuck the biker," one of them said.

The car pulled forward and I fell back against the seats. The water I'd had threatened to come back up. I tried to make myself as small as possible, not wanting to touch them. One sat on either side of me, and another across on the opposite seat. None of them seemed to pay the least bit of attention to me.

"Where are we going?" I asked.

"To your husband," said the man on my left.

My husband? I didn't think Titan had sent these men, which meant... My grandfather had sent them. Samurai was right. I'd been so stupid to leave the compound. I hadn't planned to get out of the truck, but I still shouldn't have left the safety of the fenced property. If I hadn't, I'd be safe right now, and so would Samurai.

Tears blurred my vision as I thought about him bleeding out in the parking lot. All because he'd wanted me to go back home safely to Titan. I'd messed up everything! And now I was going to be handed off to some stranger who wanted what? A wife? I doubted it. No, powerful men didn't have to buy their wives. Women flocked to them. Even if they were ugly, there were plenty of ladies who wanted them for their money alone. I just wasn't one of them.

"No more questions?" one of them asked.

The one on my right slid his hand up my thigh and gave it a squeeze. I fought not to flinch. "Maybe he won't mind if we have a little fun on the way there."

"Since those filthy bikers touched her, I don't see why it would matter," said the one across from me.

"Shut it, both of you." I glanced at the one who hadn't gotten out of the car earlier. "You really think the boss is going to want your paws all over her? Much less your cum inside her? We're getting paid for a job and we'll damn well do it."

I might not like any of these monsters, but at least one of them seemed reasonable. If they kept their hands off me, maybe it would give Titan time to figure out where I was. I didn't know how but I could hope. I didn't have a phone with me, so he couldn't track me that way. Now that I wasn't in Griffin's truck, they couldn't even call On-Star to find my location. I was well and truly screwed, which meant I had to find a way out of this on my own.

I needed to be brave.

Bravery was the last thing I was feeling. Scared. No, not just scared. I was terrified. If Titan didn't find me, what hell awaited me? Whatever man had paid for me would probably be pissed when he realized I was not only married but pregnant too. Would he force a miscarriage? Or use my child in some horrible way?

Bile rose in my throat and I whimpered, frantically trying to reach the window.

"Jesus. I think she's going to throw up. Pull over!" The man to my left banged his fist against the roof, then cut through the ropes binding me. The moment the limo came to a stop, the man opened the door and I scrambled out. My knees hit the side of the road and I immediately lost every bit of food and drink I'd had tonight.

I heard the men complaining but didn't pay them much attention. My hands shook and tears streaked my cheeks. The man who seemed the least scary dropped to his haunches next to me.

"Anything I need to know?" he asked, his voice low enough the others wouldn't hear.

I sought his gaze and what I saw shocked me. Compassion.

He looked down and noticed the ring on my finger. He lightly touched it and heaved a sigh. "Well, this is a mess. You're not just married, are you? Pregnant too?"

I nodded. He started binding my wrists again, killing what little hope I'd dared to feel.

"I take it Montcliff didn't know. How did you get yourself into this predicament?"

"He's my grandfather. He tried to sell my mother when she was younger, but she escaped him. Now he's after me and I don't know why. Please. Let me go back to my husband."

"I would if I could. My hands are just as tied as yours." Darkness entered his eyes. "He's responsible for my daughter going missing. I can't prove it, but I'm almost certain. If I screw this up, I lose my leverage."

"Would your daughter want you to sacrifice other people in order to find her?" I asked. "Just... if you can't let me go, find a way to let my husband know where I am. He's the President of Hades Abyss."

"Fuck. Montcliff screwed up this time for sure." The man shook his head. "Look, my name's Luther. I'll do what I can, but those other two? They're a different matter."

"I understand," I said.

"Eddie and Mike play by their own rules. Don't forget it. If they get you alone, they'll take what they want. And they'll get off on you fighting back."

My stomach knotted and I felt the burn in the back of my throat before I threw up again. There wasn't much left and soon I was dry heaving. By the time I got back to my feet, the reality of my situation pressed down on me. Luther couldn't let me go, and the two monsters in the car would rape me the first chance they got.

Even if they didn't, whatever man had paid for me certainly would. Because I'd never give in willingly. The only man I'd ever wanted was Titan. The thought of anyone else touching me made my skin crawl.

"I just want to go home," I said softly.

"Come on, girl," Luther said, taking my arm and putting me back into the car. "Time to go."

Whatever happened, I wouldn't break. I wouldn't give in.

Chapter Eleven

Titan

Things had gotten out of hand. I could admit it. Griffin rubbed me the wrong way. Then there was Lance and Gwen. I thought we'd won them over, but the more Griffin talked, the less certain they seemed. And I'd done the unforgiveable. I'd pushed Delilah away and yelled at her. Now I couldn't fucking find her.

"Where could she have gone?" I asked.

"She stole my truck," Griffin said, his jaw jutting out like a petulant child. "I should call the police."

Lance pulled his phone from his pocket. "First off, I bought you that truck. Second, you're not sending the police after your sister. She probably just needed to get away for a minute. We have On-Star on that vehicle. I'll call and see where it is right now."

While Lance took care of that, I shot off a text to Cache, knowing it was his turn to be on the gate. *Delilah is gone. Took her brother's truck.*

Cache texted back immediately. *Hung a right and hit the highway. Didn't know it was your woman.*

Shit. I rubbed the back of my neck. I should have known better than to let everything escalate. I was pissed at myself for letting it happen and pissed at her for leaving the compound knowing it wasn't safe out there. If I got her back in one piece, I might very well tie her ass to the bed for a month.

My phone rang with a number I didn't recognize. I answered, not knowing what to expect. "Titan."

"This is Deputy Hale. Got a man at the hospital by the name of Samurai. He's not one of yours, but before he passed out he said your name."

I remembered Hale. I'd dealt with him a few times in the past. And Samurai was one of the men from the Devil's Boneyard. If he was in the hospital, did it mean he'd followed Delilah? If so, where the hell was she?

"He's visiting from another club. What happened?"

"Shot twice and left to bleed out. He's currently in surgery. Not sure who you need to notify. Clerk inside the store said there was a young woman with him. Some men grabbed her and took off. He got a partial plate on the black limo and we're running it now," Deputy Hale said.

"Thanks. I'll touch base with Samurai's club. The woman is my wife. If you get any updates on her whereabouts…"

"I'll be sure to let you know."

I disconnected the call and squeezed the phone so tight I nearly cracked it. They'd found Delilah and I could only imagine how scared she had to be. I looked over at Lance as he hung up his call.

"They said the truck is at a gas station. I've got the address," he said.

"Won't do any good. She's not there." I reached into my pocket intending to grab my cigarettes, forgetting for a moment I'd been trying to quit and didn't have any. "Samurai followed her. He's been shot and Delilah was taken by some men in a limo. The sheriff's department is looking into it and said the clerk gave them a partial plate."

Lance cursed. "So what do we do now?"

"We either find her first, or the law will handle it. I don't know about you, but I want anyone responsible to suffer. They so much as bruise her, and I will fucking end them."

Lance nodded. "All right. Any ideas on how to find them before the police do?"

"One." I called Wizard. The phone rang several times before he answered.

"Wizard."

"It's Titan. I'm going to text you an address. Delilah took Griffin's truck to the gas station at that location. Someone snatched her from the parking lot, and they shot Samurai. My next call is to Charming, but I need you to find the men in the limo before the police do."

"On it, Pres."

He hung up and I got the address from Lance, texting it over to him. If there were any surveillance cameras in the area, I knew he'd hack them and try to locate the owner of the limo. I also knew he could access any cameras between here and wherever the limo was going, so there was a chance he could track its progress. Assuming they got near any other spots with video.

My phone rang again, with yet another number I didn't know.

"Titan."

"I need you to listen. I only have a second." I didn't recognize the man's voice, but I kept quiet to see what he had to say. "Your wife is being taken to New Orleans. That's all I can say. Don't call this number."

The line went dead, and I stared at the phone. How did that man know where Delilah was going? Was he there with her? Or had he merely seen her? I had more questions than answers, which pissed me off, but at least I had a destination. Assuming the guy hadn't outright lied to me.

There'd been a club down that way called the Broken Bastards, and I'd known their President. Also knew the guy had gone to prison and taken a shiv to the back. First, I needed to give the Devil's Boneyard an update. I scrolled through the contacts on my phone until I found what I was looking for. Then I shot off a text to Charming.

Samurai was shot. In surgery.

I had no doubt I'd get an earful about not calling with that shit, but I needed to talk to the Broken Bastards VP immediately. Assuming Breaker still *was* the VP. After the Pres had gone to prison, and been killed, I had no doubt the club had been restructured a bit. I found Breaker's name in my phone and hit the call button.

"Titan?" the man asked when he answered. "What the fuck? I haven't heard from you in years."

"Got a problem, Breaker. I was hoping your club might be willing to help. Didn't know who was the Pres down there now."

"Wrecker is the Pres now. I'm still VP. After Flame was taken out in prison, we cleaned house a bit. Found out we had a few rats. Got some new blood, and other than me, all new officers."

"You didn't want to be Pres?" I asked.

"Fuck no. I deal with enough shit already." Breaker laughed. "So what can we help with? This a paying gig, or a favor type of thing?"

"Claimed a woman. She's my wife now, and she's pregnant. Some asshole grabbed her, and I heard he's heading for New Orleans. Think she's been sold to someone down there. Need eyes on her."

"Fuck. Damn, Titan. That's just... Shit, yeah, we're all over that. Send me a photo and I'll have the club keep an eye out for her. Any clue who might have bought her?"

"I'll see if Wizard knows anything. You got any hackers down there?"

Breaker snorted. "No. My boys might be smart and cunning, but most of them aren't too great when it comes to computers."

"If Wizard needs help, there are plenty of guys to lend a hand. Give me a call if you see her. I'm going to head that way soon as I can gather some brothers."

He promised to keep me posted and we ended the call. Lance was glaring at me and I realized I hadn't shared the little tidbit about Delilah going to New Orleans. He had every right to be pissed, but the more time I spent explaining everything, the longer it would take to get down there.

I sent an update to Wizard. *Got a call. Says Delilah is going to New Orleans.*

Wizard answered almost immediately. *I'll check cameras heading that way.*

Maybe he'd have something for me before I left. I would hate to follow this lead only to discover it was total bullshit and Delilah was nowhere near New Orleans.

"I'm going," Lance said.

"Good. That means I can take my bike since you'll have your truck. Delilah shouldn't ride with me while she's pregnant. Don't want to take any chances with her or the baby." I cracked my neck. "I need to call Church and fill in the club on what's going on. Then select a few to ride with me down to New Orleans."

"Gwen will want to go. And Griffin."

"No offense, but your son isn't fucking going. If he hadn't spouted off and run his damn mouth, Delilah would still be here. Safe. He's lucky I don't put him in the ground. And your wife would only slow us down."

Lance looked like he wanted to argue, but he finally nodded his agreement and went off to talk to his family. I sent out a mass text to every member in the club. *Church in ten.*

Before I went to the clubhouse, I went to the bedroom and gathered a change of clothes for Delilah, as well as a pair of her shoes. Barney pawed my ankle. I'd forgotten all about him with all the chaos around me. I knelt down and scratched his ear.

"I'm going to bring her home, buddy."

He whined and licked my hand. I knew he'd be a comfort to Delilah when I found her and wondered how Lance would feel about a dog riding in his truck. It was only about two and a half hours to New Orleans. Barney wouldn't be too much trouble on that short of a ride.

I finished putting Delilah's things into a duffle, along with two changes of clothes for me. When I was finished, I went downstairs and tossed the bag to Lance. Gwen and Griffin were off to the side, both looking pissed as hell, but I didn't fucking care. I walked out with Barney at my heels.

"Delilah loves the dog. Can he ride with you?" I asked Lance as he stepped out of the house.

"Guess so. But you're vacuuming my truck when we get back."

I helped Barney into the vehicle. He whined when I didn't get into the truck too. After scratching behind his ear, I shut the door and got on my bike. I still had to let the club know what the hell was going on and leave Boomer in charge. The line of bikes outside the clubhouse said I was the last to arrive. I walked through the main area to the back and into Church.

"You're late to your own meeting," Boomer said with a smirk.

I flipped him off. "I'm going to make this short. Delilah is gone. Someone shot Samurai and grabbed her. Samurai is in the hospital, and Delilah is on her way to New Orleans. I'm going after her and I need a few men to ride with me. Delilah's dad is going, so we won't need anyone to drive the club truck."

"Wait. Samurai has been shot?" Stone asked.

"Yes. He was in surgery last I heard. Charming is aware of the situation. I don't expect Rooster to go with us. He needs to be here for his brother. I need Boomer here to handle any shit that comes up. Do I have any volunteers?"

"I would, Pres, but I don't want to leave MaryAnne alone," Patriot said. "She's still pretty fucked-up from being in that place."

I nodded. It was good he was looking after her.

"I'm in," said Philly.

"I'll go too," Brick said.

"Well, I can't let y'all have all the fun," Stone said.

"Three is all we can spare," I said. "I can't let anyone else from the club go with us. There's a club down there, Broken Bastards, who are going to watch out for Delilah. If they see her in town, they'll let me know where she's being held. I'm sure they'll give us a few men to help extract her."

"Reapers will probably send a few men. They're about the same distance to New Orleans as us," Wizard said. "I'm messaging Wire now."

"Tell him I'm rolling out in about ten minutes. Anyone going with me, go pack a change of clothes and meet me at the gate." Stone, Brick, and Philly walked out. "I need the rest of you to keep things running smooth here while I'm gone."

"Focus on Delilah," Boomer said. "Everything here will be fine."

I looked around the table and stood. "I'll turn it over to Boomer. Any upcoming jobs will probably have to be restructured since I'm taking some brothers with me."

I went out to my bike. Lance was idling next to it, and texting on his phone. Barney pressed his nose to the window, leaving a smear on the glass. I shook my head and smiled. I didn't know what Delilah was going through right now, or what shape I'd find her in, but I hoped the little dog would be a comfort to her.

Before I forgot, I sent a picture of Delilah over to Breaker. I didn't know if she was already in New Orleans, or if the men who took her had changed their course.

When I caught up to them, and I would no matter how long it took, I was going to make them regret ever so much as looking her way. If they'd hurt her, they'd die. Slowly and painfully.

"Hold on, baby," I muttered to myself. "I'm coming for you."

I started up the bike and pulled over to the gate, then waited for the rest of my brothers to join me. New Orleans was a two-and-a-half-hour trip, but I had a feeling I would get there in a lot less time. I'd break every law between here and there if I had to. No way I was leaving her with those men any longer than necessary. If Breaker found her before I arrived, I hoped he'd extract her if he got the chance.

My phone chimed with an incoming text.

Sending men out now to look for her.

Good. The sooner I had her back in my arms the better.

Chapter Twelve

Delilah

I'd convinced the men I needed a bathroom break, and Luther had gone with me to stand guard. It gave him the perfect opportunity to call Titan. Even though I didn't get to speak to him, at least he knew where we were going. I hoped that meant he was coming for me. Under other circumstances, I'd have enjoyed seeing New Orleans. Being held captive and threatened put a damper on things. At least Luther had kept me relatively safe.

As we approached a bricked-off property with a black metal gate, my heart slammed against my ribs. I had a feeling I wasn't going to like what we found inside. Between the brick wall and the trees hanging over the top, I couldn't see what lay behind it. Was my "husband" in there? Or my grandfather? Luther hadn't told me much. Other than our brief conversation as I threw up, and me giving him Titan's number when I used the bathroom, we hadn't had a chance to say much to one another. He'd made sure the two goons in the car with us kept their hands to themselves with sharp reminders I'd been paid for, and I was grateful to him for that much at least.

"Maybe we should have cleaned her up first," Eddie said, eyeing me.

I knew I looked a mess, but what did they expect? They'd snatched me from the gas station parking lot, and I hadn't exactly been prepared for an outing when I'd left the compound. I still wore the hideous unicorn slippers, but it was better than being barefoot. The car pulled through the gate and up to a large house. Not quite a mansion, but definitely a home owned by a very wealthy man.

The car came to a stop and Luther got out, reaching in to grab my arm and pull me from the car. The door to the house opened and a man in a three-piece suit came out, his shiny shoes clicking on the bricked walkway. An air of arrogance surrounded him. Even though he was older than me, he seemed younger than Titan. His blond hair had been brushed back and looked like it had product in it. But it was the ice-cold blue eyes that made me shiver. There wasn't an ounce of humanity in his eyes.

"Took you long enough," he said. His gaze scanned me from head to toe. "Take her inside. She'll need to be properly bathed and dressed. We're having company tonight and I want her to look her best."

"Yes, Mr. Boucher," Luther said.

Luther led me past the man and into the house. I didn't bother looking at my surroundings. It didn't matter if the house was beautiful. It was a cage. A prison. And I had no doubt I was going to die here if Titan didn't find me soon. The room Luther led me to was spacious, but I noticed there were bars across the windows. A dress had been laid across the foot of the bed, if you could call the filmy garment a dress. I eyed it, wondering exactly what I was in for tonight. Luther nudged me toward another door, and we entered a decently sized bathroom.

"Luther, why am I here?" I asked.

"On paper, you'll be Boucher's wife."

"And not on paper?" I asked.

His gaze shuttered and his lips tightened into a hard line. Right. I was essentially a whore for Boucher to use as he saw fit. I pressed a hand to my stomach, hoping I could keep my baby safe until Titan arrived. Luther reached past me into the shower stall and turned on the water, as steam filled the room he moved in closer, a hard look on his face.

"Make it seem like you're scared and disobeying," he said softly. "There are cameras and probably listening devices in here and the bedroom."

I made my eyes go wide and pressed a hand to my lips. I didn't need to feign fear. I was terrified, just not of Luther. It seemed he'd gotten tangled up in this mess as a way to save his daughter. He'd been kind to me, or as kind as he could be in this situation.

"I'll find a way to get a message to your man. Let him know where you are. I've been using a burner phone, but if Boucher gets his hands on it, he'll know I was the rat and my daughter will be lost forever. Understand?"

I gave a slight nod and took a step back, trying to act scared.

He gestured with his hands, making it seem as if he were furious with me.

"There's a group of bikers in town. Broken Bastards. Maybe I can reach out to them, see if they know your husband. Don't do anything stupid, Delilah. Boucher won't kill you quickly. He'll make you suffer." He backed up and folded his arms over his chest, nodding at the shower. "Get in."

My hands shook as I undressed, but I noticed Luther was staring at a spot just over my shoulder and not watching me. If there was a camera, like he'd said, they would think he was staring at me but I could tell otherwise. I got under the spray and cleaned myself, using quick efficient motions to get the job done as fast as possible. When I got out, Luther handed me a towel and I wrapped it around my body. He gave me another for my hair and I dried it best as I could without a hairdryer.

"I'm stepping outside the door. Don't try anything," Luther said with a stern look. "Make yourself presentable for Mr. Boucher. He'll be up shortly to see you."

Luther went out into the hall and shut the door. I heard the faint sound of a lock clicking, then the low murmur of his voice. Whoever he called, I hoped they were sending help and would get me out of here before tonight. Assuming there weren't cameras and stuff out there too. If there were, Luther could be in serious trouble.

If Boucher's friends were anything like him, tonight would be a horrific event.

I finished drying my hair and braided it. I fingered the braid, second-guessing myself. It would only give him something to easily grab. I shook my hair loose again, then pulled on the ridiculous garment. Even though it had little ties that held it closed, it was little more than a gauzy robe you could see through. Shame burned through me, knowing Boucher and anyone else in the house would see me. I might have been a webcam girl, but that had been on my terms. This was different.

Even though Boucher hadn't touched me -- yet -- I still felt violated.

I went to the window and stared out at the pretty grounds below. A room with a view. As long as I didn't mind being behind bars. Literally. I hadn't noticed any bars on the front of the house, so I had to wonder if this was the only room that had any. How long had he been planning this? Was I the first or had he taken other women against their will?

The door opened behind me and I spun, hoping it was Luther. It wasn't. Boucher walked in and shut the door behind him. He shoved his hands into his pockets and observed me, his gaze taking in every inch of my nearly exposed body.

"I'm thinking the white is no longer appropriate. Are you still untouched? I was promised you'd be a virgin, but it's been months since I brokered the deal with Montcliff." He came closer, an easy stride that said he had all the time in the world. "You can either answer truthfully, or I can find out the hard way."

My palms grew slick with sweat and my stomach rolled with nausea. He was going to rape me. Maybe do something even worse, although at the moment I couldn't think of what that might be.

"I'm not a virgin," I said softly. "I've been living with someone."

Probably best not to mention I was married to Titan and not just living with him. Although, if he'd wanted a virgin, it was doubtful his sham of a marriage was still on the table anyway.

"Pity." He came closer still and I fought the urge to run. There was nowhere to hide. He removed his hand from his pocket and reached out to cup my cheek. His touch revolted me. The tic in his jaw said he'd noticed my reaction and wasn't happy about it. "On your knees. Let's see what you've learned."

On my... I whimpered and took a step back, bumping into the window. He reached out, so fast his hand was a blur, and gripped my hair, yanking me toward him. I crashed against his chest, nearly falling to the floor.

"Tonight is going to go a little different than I'd planned. But never fear. You'll get plenty of attention, my little whore. Instead of letting my friends watch as I claim my virgin bride, I'll let them have a turn with my new toy."

I felt the burn as bile rose in my throat.

"Want to see the special room? We'll be having lots of fun in there, until my little toy is too broken." His smile was cruel. He gripped my hair tighter and used it to drag me from the room and down the stairs. We went through another door and down more stairs. At the bottom, he flicked on the lights and the horror of what I saw was enough to make me scream and battle to break free.

I kicked, hit, and struggled to get away. Boucher only laughed and seemed to enjoy my little display. He led me to a large wooden X that had shackles attached. I eyed it, fear surging through me.

"Don't like the cross?" he asked. "Did you and your boyfriend dabble with bondage?"

I shook my head, unable to speak.

He pressed me against the wooden structure and shackled my wrists, then spread my legs and fastened them in place as well. He stood back, eyes gleaming. Before I could process what he was doing, he ripped the material of my gauzy dress off my body and let the tattered pieces fall to the floor. Boucher cupped my breast, squeezing hard enough I couldn't stop the cry that rose to my lips. Tears pricked my eyes and I had no doubt he'd leave bruises.

"I think my little toy should be punished. I'd wanted a bride. Instead, I got a whore."

He walked over to another wall and opened a large wooden cabinet. The contents were beyond horrifying. Whips, chains, what looked like a branding iron, other things I didn't recognize, and lots of knives. Boucher took out a long whip, the kind I'd seen on cartoons and funny memes. He approached, flicking the end so that it made a loud snapping sound.

"Let's test your pain threshold, shall we?" he asked.

Before I could utter a word, he flicked the whip, the leather end biting into my thigh and leaving a raised welt behind. I cried out and yanked at the cuffs holding me. He did the same to the other side. Tears streaked my cheeks and I wondered if I'd live long enough for Titan to find me. What if he got here too late?

A throat cleared at the top of the stairs. "Apologies, Mr. Boucher, but there's a Mr. Satyr here to see you, as well as two of his friends."

"Satyr?" he asked, letting the whip drop to his side. "Very well. Send him down."

Send him down? As in down here with us? I felt like my lungs were constricting to the point I couldn't breathe. A loud *whooshing* filled my ears as I tried to focus on what was happening around me, although I wondered if passing out might not be better. At least then I wouldn't know what they were going to do to me.

A man in a leather cut came down the stairs, two men on his heels. *Broken Bastards MC*. Wasn't that the name of the club Luther had mentioned? Were these the men he hoped would rescue me? Or were they friends of Boucher? None of them gave me more than a quick glance before focusing on the monster in front of me.

"My invitation get lost?" Satyr asked.

"Didn't think this was your type of party," Boucher said. "Orgies are one thing, but this is another matter. But of course, if you'd like to join me..." He waved a hand at the case on the wall.

Satyr glanced at me and the intense look in his eyes only increased the tension I felt. They weren't hard and cold like Boucher's, but I didn't exactly get warm fuzzies looking at him either. The other two men came closer, their gazes locked on my face. I glanced at their cuts. *Discord* and *Bomber*.

"Pretty little thing like you would look much better on the back of a bike than on that cross," Discord said. He gave me a subtle wink and everything in me went still. Was that a message? Was he trying to tell me they were here to help?

"Perhaps I'll sell her to you when I'm finished," Boucher said.

Discord ran his fingers down my cheek. "I don't know. I may want her now. Why should I let someone else brand her? If I'm going to buy her, I'd rather she wear my marks and not yours."

I started shaking, my stomach roiling, and I couldn't stop the sobs that rose in my throat. I was going to be tortured. Raped. Probably killed. I should have never left the compound. Even worse, I'd never told Titan how I felt about him. Our child would never get the chance to be born. I couldn't see through the tears that fell rapidly, couldn't hold back any longer.

"Jesus," Discord muttered. He gripped my hair, pulling hard enough to get my attention. I tried to focus on him. "Stay with me, little girl. Woman of your standing doesn't break this easily, you hear me?"

Of my standing. I sniffled and sucked in deep breaths, trying to calm myself. When I was able to see him clearly, and I no longer felt like I was unraveling, I noticed his gaze seemed to be conveying a message. Woman of my standing. He knew! He knew I belonged to Titan.

"That's it," he crooned. "Be brave. You're strong. A fighter. Men like me don't like weak women. Understood?"

I nodded.

"I have plans for the bitch," Boucher said.

"How much?" Discord asked. "How much to walk out of here with her? She's pretty enough I want to keep her a while. You go marking up her skin and I won't pay near as much."

"I paid one hundred thousand, expecting a virgin bride. Instead, I got a whore. I'll earn my money back one way or another," Boucher said.

"You want your money? I'll pay you back the money you spent on her," Discord said. "But only if you don't touch her. I want her just as pretty as she is now, and I don't want to put my dick anywhere yours has been."

Boucher turned red, then purple. I thought he was going to attack Discord. Instead, he nodded to someone out of sight. Two men came into the room, each grabbing an arm, and hauled Discord away from me.

"Satyr, you've been to my parties, and you're welcome to stay but your friend needs to go," Boucher said. "Are the two of you going to be as problematic?"

"Nope," Satyr said.

Bomber eyed me, as if he were appraising a cow he might purchase and shook his head. "No problem here. I just want to have some fun."

"Fine, then you can both stay, as long as you keep out of my way. I need to teach this bitch a lesson." Boucher pushed them aside and stood in front of me with the whip again.

I fought not to cry out, not to scream or beg, as the leather bit into my skin again and again. He left red stripes along my ribs, across both thighs, and even across one breast, the same one he'd already bruised. Tears wet my cheeks, but I wouldn't give him the satisfaction of making a sound.

He tossed the whip aside and strode over to the cabinet. I held the gazes of Bomber and Satyr. I'd have missed the clue if I hadn't been paying attention. Bomber shoved his hand into his denim pocket, then untucked three fingers. He tapped them twice before shifting again and crossing his arms.

Three. Three what? Three minutes? Hours? Three more men were coming?

Boucher approached me again. The blade of the knife he held gleamed under the lights. He tightened his grip on it before reaching for me. His fingers closed over my hair and wrenched my head to the side. I heard him sawing through the locks as he tossed down one handful after another of my hair. When he was finished, the strands didn't even brush my shoulders.

He pressed the knife to my throat and leaned in close. "Did your boyfriend like all that hair? I just might shave your head when I'm finished with you, before I throw your ass into the nearest whorehouse. Men won't care if you have hair on your head. Long as they can put their dick in you, that's all that matters."

The monster smiling at me terrified me more than anything else I'd ever seen. I'd never known a man like him before. Or rather, I hadn't realized I had. It seemed my grandfather was just as evil as this bastard.

Boucher walked off again, coming back with a branding iron and what I assumed was a blowtorch. Shit. There was no way I could survive that without passing out or screaming. I felt my heart start to race, and my gaze darted around the room, hoping for a rescue or escape of some kind.

A crash sounded upstairs, and Bomber winked at me.

Was that what we'd been waiting for? Had he known someone was coming to save me?

I heard the frantic barking of a dog, shouts, and gunfire. Boucher cursed and tossed aside the items in his hand. He grabbed another knife, this one bigger than the last, and came for me. He drew his arm back, the knife over his head. Before he could bring it down and impale me with it, the barking got louder. I heard a vicious growl and a blur of fawn-colored fur shot toward me, latching onto Boucher's leg.

"Barney?" Where had the little corgi come from?

Boucher tried to shake him free, cursing and hopping. He kicked at the dog, but Barney came right back. His fangs flashed, and his growls filled the air. While he kept Boucher busy, Bomber freed me from the cuffs holding me to the cross. He shrugged out of his cut and yanked his shirt over his head, quickly tugging it over mine and covering my body. Bomber put his cut back on and took my hand.

"Come on, beautiful. Let's get you out of here."

He led me to the stairs, and I froze. "Titan?"

He took the last few steps and crushed me to him, breathing me in. I felt a tremor run through him and tried not to cry out from the pain of being held so tight. I was safe. He'd come for me!

"Stay with Bomber, Delilah."

I shook my head. "I'm not leaving without you."

He gave me tight-lipped smile and nodded. "All right, but you may not like what you see."

He moved farther into the room, calling off Barney. The little corgi ran to me, pressing against my ankles. I knelt and wrapped my arms around him.

"My hero," I murmured as I buried my face in his fur.

Titan gripped Boucher by his neck, lifting him off the floor. "You sent men after my wife? Kidnapped her. Hurt her. Biggest fucking mistake you've ever made."

"Wife?" Boucher asked in a choked voice.

"Yes." Titan smiled, but it was cold and hard. "Wife. And the mother of my child. I will fucking end you, but not before you suffer."

"Did he rape you? Before we got here?" Bomber asked softly.

"No. I think he planned to, but he hadn't gotten there yet. He'd just started when you arrived."

"Titan, he hurt her but he didn't rape her," Bomber called out.

"Doesn't fucking matter. He would have." My husband carried Boucher by his throat and pressed him to the cross I'd been shackled to. Satyr fastened the man in place, then Titan used the discarded knife to slice the man's clothes off. My husband smirked at Boucher's cock. "That why you have to rape women? Hell, if it got any smaller, it would disappear."

Boucher turned purple again and sputtered, but kept his mouth shut. He must have realized how dire his situation was.

"Let me be clear," Titan said. "There's no one coming to rescue you. And no one will ever find your body. You're simply going to disappear."

"You can't do this," Boucher said, a whine to his voice.

"Oh, I can. And I will," Titan said. His gaze swung to hold mine. "Last chance, baby. Leave before I get started. You won't be able to unsee what happens down here. I don't ever want you to see me with that much blood on my hands."

Bomber tugged on my arm. "Come on. He's right. You don't need to watch."

I let him lead me up the stairs and away from Titan. But the screams that followed me I knew would live in my nightmares for weeks to come.

Chapter Thirteen

Titan

Satyr stood at my side, arms folded, as he observed Boucher with a bored look on his face. I'd be forever in the debt of the Broken Bastards for getting to Delilah and hopefully delaying the worst of her torture until I'd been able to arrive. The little pissant in front of me deserved to die, but I wasn't going to let him go anytime soon. I wanted to draw this out.

I stripped off my cut and pulled my shirt over my head, not wanting to get blood on either. Satyr gripped my arm, staring at the ink on my bicep. I knew the moment he saw what was hidden in the various bits of art. Most people didn't look close enough.

"Semper Fi," he murmured and let me go.

I stared at him, and he tugged down the collar on his tee. A devil dog was inked on his pectoral. I gave him a nod, then focused on Boucher.

"Marine?" Boucher asked, his eyes going wide and darting between me and Satyr. "You're both Marines?"

"Guess you fucked up bad," I said. I picked up the branding iron and blowtorch. "Now what were you going to do with these?"

"Nothing!" Boucher struggled against his restraints.

"Kept calling your woman a whore. Said he was going to sell her to a whorehouse when he was finished because men didn't care what she looked like as long as they could put their dicks in her." Satyr narrowed his eyes at Boucher. "If I find out any of the parties I attended here had unwilling women, I'll bring you back from the dead just so I can kill you myself.

Never raped a woman in my life and the thought I may have unknowingly done so turns my stomach."

I turned on the torch and used it to heat the end of the branding iron. When it glowed red, I pressed it to Boucher's abdomen, making him scream and thrash. The scent of burned flesh would have bothered a lesser man, but this wasn't my first round with torture. I used the branding iron to leave four more marks on his torso and thighs. He blubbered and begged, as if it would make a difference.

"I'll leave her alone," he said. "You'll never hear from me again."

"You're right. I won't because you'll be buried six feet under."

Satyr cleared his throat. "We don't bury our dead in the ground. Best to take him to the swamp and feed him to the gators."

I paused. "You don't bury them?"

Satyr shrugged a shoulder. "New Orleans is below sea level. We bury everyone aboveground. Doesn't exactly help with hiding a body, unless you put him in an old crypt no one visits anymore. You could toss him into the coffin with the bones of whoever is resting there. As long as the smell didn't draw attention, it's possible he'd never be found."

Interesting. "I think the gators are a better option."

Boucher had paled considerably. He slumped against his restraints and I knew he'd finally accepted his fate. Fucker should have left Delilah alone.

"Titan." I turned at the sound of Stone's voice. "Found two girls up here. Not even eighteen yet."

"What did he do to them?" I asked.

"Raped them. Not just him either," Stone said. "One's in really bad shape. The other is spitting mad.

Keeps hissing at us like a fierce little kitten. Got most of my information from her."

I eyed Boucher, then yelled up to Stone. "Bring down the angry one. Make sure the other one has whatever medical care she needs."

The soft tread of steps told me the girl was on her way. She wore a T-shirt I recognized as Stone's, and fire flashed in her eyes as she stared at Boucher. She spat in his face.

"He's going to pay the ultimate price for what he did to you, and what he intended for my wife," I said. "But I wanted you to see him like this, to know he can't ever hurt you again."

Her gaze swung to me, then dropped to the knife on the floor. What happened next was enough to make even me cringe and cup my balls. She stabbed Boucher twice in the gut before driving the knife straight between his legs. The sound he made was inhuman and the blood flowed freely before he passed out. Pity. I'd wanted him alive when he bled out, to feel every excruciating second.

She backed up and I noticed she was trembling. Stone came down the stairs, took one look at her, and wrapped his arm around her shoulders, leading her back to the main part of the house. It seemed he'd won her over. Whatever he'd said, it had gotten her down here, and she wasn't fighting to get away from him.

"Fuck. That was both scary and hot at the same time," Satyr said.

"Boucher pissed off the wrong woman," I said. I found a small sink across the room and rinsed the blood off before I put my shirt and cut back on. I noticed a bunch of hair on the floor and thought I saw streaks of purple. "Or girl. Stone said she wasn't even eighteen yet. I can only imagine the hell she's been through. The kill should have been hers. I just didn't think she'd want to do it."

"My club will handle the cleanup," Satyr said. "Wrecker has a friend with the local police. He can smooth things over if necessary. Go take care of your woman."

I clapped him on the shoulder before heading upstairs. Delilah was outside in her father's truck, Barney in her lap. Her haunted eyes focused on me as I hurried toward her. I yanked the truck door open and wrapped her in my arms, Barney smooshed between us, not that the furry beast seemed to care.

"I could have lost you," I murmured.

"You got here in time," she said.

"Not quite," Lance said. "She needs medical care."

Bomber appeared almost out of nowhere. "We have a doc at the clubhouse. Bring her there and he can treat her."

"Appreciate it," I said.

"I'll follow you." Lance buckled his seatbelt. "Do we need to find a hotel for the night?"

"No!" Delilah looked almost panicked as she latched onto me. "I want to go home, Titan. Please."

I nodded. "If you think you can handle the trip home, that's what we'll do. Let's have the doc take a look first, okay?"

"Okay," she said softly.

I brushed a kiss against her forehead, then shut the door. After I started up my bike, I pulled down the drive and out the gate. Three Broken Bastards were in front of me leading the way, and another took up the rear with my brothers. Their compound was outside the city heading into the swamplands, and nowhere near as big as mine. They had a barbed-wire fence around the place and hadn't even bothered with a gate. The clubhouse looked rickety on the outside, made of what appeared to be driftwood.

A long porch ran across the front and Breaker stood on the steps, the glow of a cigarette announcing his presence even in the darkness before I could make out his features. I parked next to Lance's truck and helped Delilah from the vehicle. Barney leapt down and immediately started marking his territory. While he was occupied, I took Delilah inside, hoping like hell they didn't have club whores all over the damn place.

My hopes were dashed the second we walked inside. Women ran around naked. Some were giving blowjobs or getting fucked outright. I glanced at Breaker, who only shrugged and motioned for me to go straight through the crowd. I lifted Delilah into my arms. After all she'd been through, I didn't know how she was upright. Didn't matter. I wasn't about to let her walk barefoot through whatever might be on the floor in here. When I reached the other side of the room, Breaker pointed to the stairs.

We went up to the second floor and into the only room that stood open. The place looked bigger inside than it had from out front. And the interior wasn't as shabby as the outside appeared. A full-size bed was in the middle of the room with a chair beside it. The only other furniture in the room was a dresser with a small TV on top. Another door opened to a small bathroom.

I eased Delilah onto the bed.

"Don't worry. It's clean," said a man from the doorway. "I'm Turbo."

I shook his hand, glancing at his cut. *Sergeant-at-Arms.*

"Turbo is a man of many talents," Breaker said. "Served as a medic in the Army and even went to medical school."

"Decided I hate school." Turbo grinned. "But I'm decent at patching people up. Heard your woman had a rough time of it with Boucher. Hope you killed that fucker."

"Actually, one of his victims had that honor. Found two girls in the house. One was in bad shape. The other was pissed as hell."

"Luther," Delilah said. "He said my grandfather was responsible for his daughter going missing. But if he was at Boucher's place, then he must have thought his daughter was there."

"Could be one of them is his daughter," I said. "I didn't stop to ask. He's the one who tipped off the Broken Bastards, but I didn't pay much attention to him when I got there."

"Where exactly are you hurt?" Turbo asked Delilah.

"My thighs, abdomen, and..." Her cheeks burned a bright pink. I gave Lance a nod to head out and he stepped into the hall, along with Breaker.

"It's okay, baby. Where did he hurt you?" I asked.

She touched her breast. "I think he bruised me, and he used a whip on me."

I growled and shut my eyes, wishing I could bring the fucker back to life just so I could kill him all over again. I'd let the girl have that honor, but now I wished I'd ended his life. Either way, he'd never harm another woman ever again. It would have to be enough.

I helped Delilah remove the shirt Bomber had given her, my body blocking her from Turbo's gaze.

After I helped her arrange it so most of her was covered, I stepped back so he could take a look at her wounds. He grabbed an old-fashioned doctor's bag from beside the dresser, one I hadn't even noticed until now, and opened it up. His touch seemed gentle as he treated the welts and cuts she'd sustained. She'd been right about the bruising. I could see fingermarks on her breast where the asshole had grabbed her.

"She got off easy," he said. "Not that I'm belittling what Delilah went through, but it could have been much worse. She'll heal within a week."

"Is it safe for her to ride back to Mississippi tonight?" I asked. "She said she wanted to go home."

"Can't blame her." Turbo smiled. "As long as the car ride isn't too rough, she should be fine. I can give her something for pain before you leave."

"She's pregnant," I said.

"Then I'll make sure it's something safe for the baby. Sit tight and I'll see what I can find. Do you need anything?" Turbo asked.

"There's a duffle in her dad's truck. It has a set of clothes for her."

Turbo nodded. "I'll bring it up with me when I return."

He shut the door behind him, and I sank onto the edge of the mattress, reaching for Delilah's hand. I couldn't remember a time I'd been more scared than when she'd been taken. When Phoebe had been snatched, I hadn't realized she was my daughter. It wasn't until later that we found out. Still, as much as I loved my kid and my grandkids, having Delilah disappear like she had was a terror I never wanted to feel again.

"There's something I need to tell you," I said, running my fingers over her palm. "I didn't even realize it until you were gone. Finding out you were missing, and that someone had taken you… it tore me up, Delilah. And it made me realize how much I love you."

I heard her indrawn gasp. "You love me?"

I nodded.

Tears misted her eyes as she reached up to cup my cheek. "I love you too. It's the one regret I had when I realized Boucher was probably going to kill me. I'd never gotten to tell you how I felt, or rather I'd been too scared to admit it."

"You know I'm not letting you leave the compound alone again. At least, not for a good year or two. It will take that long for me to stop worrying every time you aren't in my line of sight."

She leaned closer and brushed her lips against mine. "I'm okay with that."

Turbo came back with a bottle of water and some pills, as well as the duffle from the truck. After making sure Delilah took the medication, he left so she could get dressed. I helped her into her clothes and ran my fingers through her much shorter hair. The ends were jagged, and I remembered the hair I'd seen on the floor at Boucher's. I'd been so focused on getting Delilah out of there, I hadn't really thought about the hair being hers.

"He cut your hair off." I touched the ends again.

"I'll need to get it cleaned up so it doesn't look so awful. He hacked it off with a knife. I'm sure it's uneven and… and… ugly."

"Baby, you could never look ugly. It doesn't matter how long your hair is. It will grow back, or you may decide you like it short. I don't care as long as you like it." I kissed her again, my lips caressing hers. "Come on, beautiful. Let's go home."

I stood and lifted her into my arms, carrying her down to her dad's truck. Lance must have heard we were leaving because he was already waiting with the engine running. Or he'd seen more than he wanted at the clubhouse. I had a feeling he'd have a few questions for me later. Once Delilah was buckled, I put Barney in the truck and shut the door. I got on my bike and pulled away from the Broken Bastards clubhouse, thankful for their help. I'd make sure they were compensated for their part in Delilah's rescue.

It took two hours to get back home, and when we pulled up to my house, Gwen was standing on the porch. I knew Lance must have called her. I was grateful to see Griffin wasn't with her. I parked my bike under the carport and picked up Delilah from the front seat of the truck. Barney jumped to the ground and raced to the front door, apparently just as happy to be home as my wife was.

"Door is unlocked," I said as I went up the steps.

Gwen pushed it open, letting Barney into the house, and I followed. I eased Delilah onto the couch in the living room and took a step back. Her mom immediately rushed to her side, holding her tight.

"I'm so sorry, baby," Gwen said, tears sliding down her cheeks. "I never meant to make you feel like you had to leave your own home, and I know Griffin feels the same way. Things got out of hand."

"Gwen, honey, I think she'd like some time alone with Titan," Lance said. "Maybe we can come for breakfast in the morning or meet in town for lunch."

Gwen nodded, hugging Delilah one more time before she stood.

I saw them out, shutting and locking the door behind them. No matter how well-meaning anyone might be, I didn't want any interruptions tonight.

"Come on, baby. You want to lie down?" I asked.

"Will you stay with me?"

I knelt at her feet, taking her hands in mine. "I'm not leaving your side for any longer than necessary."

I stood and picked her up, carrying her upstairs to our bedroom. Barney stayed at my feet and stretched out on the floor next to the bed. I helped Delilah into a nightgown, then turned down the covers. She slid into bed as I stripped out of my clothes. I looked down at myself and paused. I'd gotten the blood off at Boucher's, but I didn't want to risk having missed any spots. No fucking way would I get into bed before I knew for sure I'd gotten it all.

"I should shower," I said.

"Leave the door open?" she asked.

"Of course. I'll be quick." I went into the bathroom and started the shower, not even waiting for the water to warm. I scrubbed my skin and hair with brisk motions, rinsed, and got out. I toweled off, then went back to the bedroom, where Delilah lay curled on her side of the bed. She held out a hand to me and I slid in next to her, pulling her into my arms.

"Don't ever let me go," she murmured, clinging to me.

"Never." I pressed my lips to her forehead, then her lips. "You're mine. Now and always. There's no one I love more than you."

She looked up at me, her lower lip trembling. "Make love to me, Justin. Please. Wipe away the memory of his hands on me. I need something happy, something good, to focus on."

"Baby, I don't want to hurt you." I lightly ran my hand down her side. "You're injured."

"It doesn't matter. I need you."

I kissed her, trying to take things slow. I gathered her nightgown as my lips moved over hers. I pulled back to remove the garment, leaving her naked in my arms. The feel of her curves against my body was enough to make my already hard cock stiffen even more.

I rolled us so that I lay on my back with Delilah draped over me. "Better this way, baby. You take the lead. Take what you need from me."

Her gaze locked with mine as she straddled me, her slick pussy brushing against my cock. I gripped my shaft while she sank down onto it, groaning at how fucking incredible she felt. I placed my hands on her hips but tried not to hold on too tight.

"Ride me, beautiful."

It was all the urging she needed. Delilah rose and fell, each stroke taking me deeper until she'd taken every inch I had to give. Her movements were slow. She splayed her hands on my chest, giving her better leverage.

"That's it. Fuck but you feel good." I reached between us, rubbing her clit.

Delilah cried out. Her hips jerked and soon she was riding me faster, pushing both of us to the brink. I worked her clit until she screamed out my name, her pussy milking my cock. I bucked my hips, thrusting up into her as I came.

She panted for breath and collapsed on my chest. Running my hand up and down her back, I felt my cock twitch inside her. "I didn't hurt you, did I?"

"No. It was wonderful, and just what I needed." She pressed kisses to my chest before kissing my lips. "Love you, Justin."

"Love you too, baby."

She fell asleep in my arms, our bodies still joined. Now that I had her back, I was never letting her go. I was protective of her before, but now I was going to take it up a few notches. I'd assign someone to her twenty-four hours a day, every day of the fucking week. Every time she left the house, she'd have a shadow. Maybe two.

"You're my entire world, baby," I murmured. "My everything."

Epilogue

Delilah -- One Month Later

I sat in the kitchen, my heel on the edge of my chair as I painted my toenails. Barney snored on the floor nearby, and I heard Titan talking on the phone in the other room. Neither of my guys left my side for long. Titan had gotten word my grandfather was no longer an issue, but he still didn't let me leave without at least two bodyguards. I wasn't sure who had been more scared the day I'd been taken. Me or him.

He came back into the room, but I heard another set of booted steps behind him. I craned my neck to see who else was here and leapt out of my seat when I saw Samurai.

"You're all right!" I threw my arms around him, making him grunt. "Sorry! Sorry. I didn't mean to hurt you."

"I'm fine. Just still a bit tender," he said. "My club is sending someone to get my bike and I'll ride back in the truck."

"Thank you. For coming after me that day." I kissed his cheek, earning me a growl from Titan. "I'm glad you're okay. When I saw you on the ground that night, and all the blood, I thought you were dead."

"I'm tougher than that." He smiled. "I just wanted to come say goodbye. Try to stay out of trouble."

I nodded and leaned back against Titan as he pulled me against his body. Samurai walked out and I heard the front door shut a moment later.

"He's not the only one on the mend," Titan said. "Galahad and Morgan are going to be fine too. Morgan's broken bones have healed, and Galahad is about back to normal. And I heard the two girls we found at Boucher's are both recovering nicely. One of them was Luther's daughter, and the other had been living on the streets. But they're going to be okay."

"Does this mean we get our happily-ever-after now?" I asked.

"Is this a storybook?" He sounded amused and I tipped my head back, noting the smile on his lips.

"Well, I did have a sexy hero come rescue me. I might not be a princess, but it doesn't mean we can't live our own fairy tale. Besides, a big, badass biker is way better than a prince."

He leaned down and kissed me. "I'm glad you feel that way."

"What's next?"

"Next?" he asked.

"For us. For the club. The bad guys have been dealt with. So what happens now?" I asked.

"You already said what happens."

I turned in his arms and looped my arms around his neck. "I did?"

He grinned. "Yeah. We live happily ever after."

Rising on my tiptoes, I kissed him soft and slow. He gripped my hips lifting me and I wound my legs around his waist. Barney barked at our feet and I couldn't help but laugh.

"I don't think he likes you manhandling me."

"Then he can go outside," Titan said. "Because you're mine. My wife. My love. The very breath in my lungs."

I melted a little at his words. "You say the sweetest things."

He dipped his head, his voice going a bit lower. "Don't tell anyone. You'll ruin my image. I'm supposed to be the President of Hades Abyss, untouchable, unshakeable. If everyone knows my wife has me wrapped around her finger, I may be overthrown."

I couldn't help but laugh. "Now you're being silly. Who on earth would dare try to take down Titan?"

The smile slipped from his face. "Someone, somewhere. My life will never be safe or ordinary, Delilah. There will always be danger lurking in the shadows, coming for me when I least expect it. But I will give my life to keep you safe. You and our child. That's a vow I'll never break."

"Then we should enjoy the peace and quiet while we have some." I nipped his bottom lip. "Or maybe we can go make some noise of our own."

"Insatiable," he murmured.

"Only because of the sexy beast I get to call my husband. He's the only man I've ever wanted, *will* ever want. Because I love him above all others."

Titan kissed me, our lips not breaking apart even as he carried me upstairs, shutting the door before Barney could dart into our room. I didn't know what tomorrow would bring, any more than he did, but I knew I'd love him until I drew my last breath. I'd come here to find my independence. I never counted on finding love.

In Titan, I had a husband. A lover. And a best friend. Everything I'd ever wanted. Maybe this wasn't happily-ever-after, but it was close enough for me.

Titan (Hades Abyss MC 5)
Deleted Scene
Harley Wylde

What happened when Titan sent Patriot to get MaryAnne? Find out in this deleted scene…

Deleted Scene

Patriot

I eyed the building in front of me and wondered why the fuck the Pres had thought this would be a good place for MaryAnne. Or any human. It looked like a prison. A neglected one. Or maybe one of those asylums from the nineteenth century. It wouldn't surprise me if the place was haunted. From what I'd seen of the abuse MaryAnne had suffered here, I didn't doubt for a second the "doctors" had gone too far more than once and killed their patients. Did the victims still roam the halls?

Get it together. This isn't a fucking novel.

I went inside, stopping in the lobby. It seemed nice enough from here. A pretty woman smiled at me, and two guards glowered from nearby.

"May I help you?" she asked.

"I'm here to get MaryAnne Swenson." I pulled out the paperwork Wire had "created" and handed it over. The woman looked it over, tapped on her computer for a few minutes, then picked up the phone and whispered to whomever was on the other end of the line.

I heard a click and glanced over at the door in the corner. I'd noticed it when I walked in. In addition to the two guards out there, the door itself had a scanner lock that required a badge to gain access. A doctor hurried out, his brow furrowed, and irritation flashing in his eyes. "What's this about MaryAnne Swenson being removed from this facility?" the doctor demanded.

I eyed his ID badge. *Dr. Gregory Jones.* "Dr. Jones, I gave the lady at the desk the proper paperwork. MaryAnne is leaving. Today. If you refuse to release her into my care, you won't be happy with the consequences."

The doctor puffed up. "And what might those be?"

I leaned in closer, dropping my voice so only he could hear. "How about a leak to the media of the footage you recorded of MaryAnne being raped by multiple guards? Or the ice bath you forced her into when she became hysterical after the incident? Perhaps you'd prefer they see the video of you charging men to use her like a damn whore." I backed up a step and watched with satisfaction as the doctor paled considerably. He swayed a moment before clearing his throat, straightening his coat, and giving the order to have MaryAnne brought to the front.

"Oh, fuck no. You think I'm trusting you or anyone here? The only one getting MaryAnne will be me," I said. "Now open that fucking door and show me where she is."

I followed the asshole through the rat maze until he stopped at a metal door. He unlocked it and I heard the whimpering inside. I shoved him out of the way and opened the door, my eyes adjusting to the dim interior. MaryAnne huddled on a cot in the corner, her arms around her knees, as she rocked back and forth. And she was completely fucking naked.

I snarled at the doctor and grabbed him by the throat. "What the fuck?"

He couldn't answer. His face started to turn purple as he gasped and wheezed. I wanted to rip the fucker to pieces but settled for slamming him into the wall several times until he slumped to the floor -- knocked out cold.

The sound in the room had stopped. I watched MaryAnne, and she watched me in return.

"Sweetheart, my name is Patriot and I'm with the Hades Abyss MC. Your cousin, Sean, is one of my brothers in the club. He goes by Galahad now. I'm here to take you home."

She didn't freak out, but she didn't exactly move closer to me either. I stepped into her room, moving slow and steady. The first sign she was freaked out, I'd back the hell up, but I needed to get her out of this hellhole. I shrugged out of my cut and pulled my shirt over my head. Her body tensed and she stared with wide eyes. I held the shirt out to her.

"For you. Cover up, baby. Not taking you out of here naked."

She reached for the shirt, only her fingertips touching it before she quickly yanked it from my hand and pulled it over her head. I put my cut back on and reached for her. When she didn't scream or run away, I lifted her into my arms and cradled her close to my chest. "Time to leave, MaryAnne. And you will never fucking come back here again."

She clung to me. I made sure the shirt covered her ass as I carried her back to the front and out of the building. I had almost brought my bike, but I hadn't been sure what condition she'd be in when I got here. Now I was glad I had my old Bronco since she didn't have any clothes.

I unlocked the passenger door and eased her down onto the seat. I pulled the seatbelt across her. "Got to keep you safe."

She burst into tears and reached for me. I hugged her best I could with her restrained in the seat and let her cry it out. I didn't know what I'd said to bring on the flood, but if anyone had earned the right to fall apart it was her. "Get it all out, sweetheart."

When she sniffled and the tears slowed, I pulled back and wiped her cheeks. "Ready to go home?"

She nodded.

I shut the door and went around to the driver's side then climbed in. The engine rumbled to life, the big beast noisy as fuck, but that's part of what I loved about it. That and the sheer size. The 1990 Bronco Custom was wider than most vehicles, and I'd had it lifted, so it was a monster. "You're in for a bumpy ride," I warned.

Her large eyes were still glassy, but the smile she gave me about knocked the air from my lungs. God but she was stunning.

I put the truck in gear and pulled away from her prison. I knew Wire was planning something for that place, and I hoped like hell he made sure every one of those sick fuckers paid a high price for what they'd done to MaryAnne and who knew how many others.

Whatever it took for her to feel safe, I'd make sure she got it.

Grease Monkey -- A Bad Boy Romance
Harley Wylde

For all appearances, Gwen's daddy's little darling -- a socialite with more money than sense -- but what she really wants is to break free from her gilded cage.

When her Mercedes breaks down, Gwen's knight in shining tow trucks turns out to be more than she expected. Will the hot mechanic be the first guy to rock her world? She melts at his touch and knows that she'll give him whatever he wants, as long as he keeps her screaming his name.

Chapter One

Gwen

I could count on one hand the number of times I'd been told *no* and had someone actually mean it. I was spoiled, rotten to the core, and daddy's little darling. Or at least, that's what the world saw when they looked at me. A perfect little blonde China doll driving around town in the Mercedes Daddy gave her. They don't see the ugliness of my life, the harsh reality of being a Montcliff. Appearance is everything after all. All the women wanted to be me and all the guys wanted to fuck me, and that was a card my daddy never hesitated to play.

Any time he had a big client on the line, I was the one he sent to wine and dine them. I was waiting for the day he sold me to the highest bidder. I knew it was coming, now that I've refused to finish college. I don't have a problem expanding my education, but the last thing I wanted to study was business, and Daddy was cramming it down my throat, wanting to groom me to be the perfect wife for one of his associates, and I was sure I knew which one. Lecherous old man.

I'd been driving aimlessly for over an hour, my mind in a whirl over my latest fight with Daddy dearest, and it didn't take a genius to realize I was lost. I hadn't been home in years and had never driven in Winston Falls before. My New England town was beautiful, though, and I'd wanted to go exploring before anyone could fasten a leash to my collar this morning. The fall leaves had been gorgeous, but at some point, I'd left behind the mansions of Piper Hill and, well... the houses and businesses around me weren't falling apart, but they definitely belonged to the lower class.

I snorted. *Lower class.* Now I sounded like my snobby as hell mother, if you could call her that. My real mother had died giving birth to me, and my father hadn't wasted time remarrying. He'd been through four wives since then, and his latest was only a few years older than me. It seemed every time he got married, the woman got a little younger. Pretty soon, he'd be bride shopping at the boarding school where I spent most of my life. The thought sickened me, but I knew he wasn't above it. Knowing the sick bastard, he'd probably get off on having a child bride. Someone he could groom to his liking.

My car gave a clunk and rattle before the entire thing shimmied. "No. No, no, no. You aren't doing this to me now!"

I stared at the gauge and wondered how the hell I'd managed to run out of gas. I was always careful about making sure I had a full tank, but apparently, I'd fucked up this time. I didn't even remember the last gas station I'd seen, not that I had a gas can stored in my trunk. The only thing back there was my latest shopping haul. As far as I knew, I didn't even have a car jack back there, but then I'd always called roadside service if I had a flat.

The car sputtered to a stop in the middle of the road, and I banged my head on the steering wheel. What the hell had I ever done wrong for the universe to hate me so much? I picked up my cell phone and stared at the black screen. I tried to power it on and realized my battery had died. Searching through the console and glove compartment, I couldn't find the charger. I must have taken it out of the car at some point. Great. Stranded. It was a long-ass walk back home, especially in heels. With my luck, someone would think I was a high priced call girl and try to pick me up along the way.

A loud roar reached my ears and I glanced in the rearview mirror. About six motorcycles were barreling my way. I hoped like hell they didn't stop to check on me. It wasn't that I had anything against guys who rode motorcycles, but six rowdy men and just one of me? The odds weren't in my favor. They whizzed past and I let out a breath I hadn't realized I was holding. Minutes ticked by as I tried to assess my situation and figure out what the hell I was going to do. I could have walked, but to where? I wasn't familiar with this part of town and would be just as lost on foot.

I heard the rumble of a big engine behind me and looked in my rearview mirror again. Was that a tow truck? Maybe my day wasn't complete crap after all. It seemed miracles did still happen, even if they seldom ever happened to me. Whoever he was, surely he would be able to take me to the nearest gas station, and I could just fill up my car and be on my way. I had a little cash on me, but with some luck, they wouldn't take checks or plastic.

I opened my door and swung my legs out before rising to meet my savior. Probably a good thing I was holding onto the doorframe when the driver stepped out. Holy mother of God! My knees went a little weak as a giant of a man moved toward me, his muscles bunching and flexing with every step. Mirrored sunglasses hid his eyes, but I got the feeling he was assessing me. Jeans were molded to his thick thighs, and a grease-stained white tee stretched tight over his massive chest and shoulders. My tongue stuck to the roof of my mouth as he stopped in front of me.

"You look like you could use some help."

His deep voice sent shivers down my spine, and my cheeks burned as my panties grew damp. Holy fuck! I'd be willing to bet he could get a woman off just using his voice. And for the first time in my life, I was ready to volunteer to be that woman. No man had ever turned me on before. At school, the boys at the school across town had referred to me as the ice princess. I hadn't even been able to get myself off, so I'd thought maybe they were right. Until now.

His eyebrows rose, and I realized I hadn't said anything.

"It died in the middle of the road." I licked my lips. "I ran out of gas."

"I can take it back to my garage and take a look. It's just a few blocks away." He held out his hand. "Name's Lance."

I couldn't stop the giggle that bubbled up.

"Something wrong with my name?"

"Sorry, it's just... with you swooping in to rescue me and your name... it made me think of Lancelot."

He smiled a little, the corner of his lips ticking upward. My legs squeezed together as more moisture gathered between my thighs. I'd never felt so needy before, so out of control. If he kept talking, I was going to hump his leg in the middle of the street, maybe beg him to fuck me over the hood of my car. I was practically salivating as I moved a little closer.

"So if I'm Lancelot, does that make you Guinevere?"

He pulled his glasses down his nose, and there was humor shining in his gray eyes. Gorgeous eyes. A sigh escaped me, and I had to stop myself from rubbing against him like a cat in heat. He seemed to realize the effect he had on me and smirked as he slid his glasses back into place.

"All right, Gwennie. Let's get your car, and you, back to my shop."

Hearing the nickname on his lips ratcheted my need up another notch. Little did he know he wasn't far off from my real name.

"I actually just need gas, if you could get me to a service station?"

If anything, he looked even more amused. "Do you not know that running out of gas can do all sorts of damage to your car? It's better to haul it back to my place and take a look. No guarantee putting gas in it will work."

Who was I to argue with an expert on the subject? I handed him my keys, and he walked me around to the passenger side of his truck. My knight opened the door for me, and I stared up at the truck and then down at my dress. I gathered the skirt in my hands and hiked it up before stepping up into the monster vehicle. When I looked back at Lance, his eyes were glued to my ass. Maybe the attraction wasn't one-way then. He gave me a sexy little smirk before closing the door.

By the time he slipped behind the wheel to pull in front of my car, I had thought I had my raging hormones under control. The tattoos snaking down his arms made me shiver in the best of ways. The only guys I'd been around were clean cut in polos and khakis. This guy with his ink, abs of steel, and that sexy as fuck beard were the exact opposite of every guy who'd ever tried to get in my pants. Maybe it wasn't so much that I'd been an ice princess all my life. Maybe I'd just needed someone a little bad, a little dirty, and all kinds of sexy to rev my engine.

He got out and started the process of getting my car loaded onto his truck bed.

I let out a little moan as I pictured the two of us together, our chemistry off the charts as he drove us back to his shop. Maybe he'd get me off and then I'd unzip his pants and return the favor. I'd always wondered what it felt like to suck a cock. I'd read a few romance novels in my day, and the heroines always seemed to enjoy it. I bit my lip, suddenly wanting to taste Lance more than I'd ever wanted anything. A more confident woman, a more worldly woman, would know how to seduce him.

After he had my car on the back of his truck and he slid back behind the wheel, I hugged the door, afraid I'd maul him if given the opportunity. The last thing he probably needed was some virgin socialite attacking him while he was driving. The man could probably have any woman he wanted, so why the hell he would want me?

"I don't bite," he said, eyeing me across the cab of the truck.

"I know."

He looked amused, his lips tipping up. "So you're hugging the door because…"

I looked down at my white-knuckled grip on the handle and let go. I tried to relax back into the seat, but the uncomfortable ache between my legs continued to grow. My panties were soaked, and I wondered if my dress was getting wet too. Was I going to leave a wet spot on the seat of his truck? My cheeks flamed as my nipples hardened at the thought, poking through the top of my dress.

I couldn't see his eyes behind the mirrored glasses, but something told me he'd noticed my body's reaction. I couldn't help but drop my gaze to his crotch, and a gasp slipped past my lips at the rather large bulge behind his zipper. My heart raced, and I quivered, wanting him more than I'd ever wanted anything.

"You keep looking at me like that, princess, and we're going to be delayed getting to the shop."

"Like what?" I asked breathlessly.

"Like you want to eat me up. Or maybe you want me to eat you?" He smirked a little. "Is that it, princess? You picturing my mouth between those creamy thighs of yours?"

"Oh, God." I moaned and squeezed my legs tighter together.

"I run a full service station, sweetheart. I'd be happy to take the edge off."

He couldn't mean…"What?"

"Why don't you slide that pretty little ass over here?"

My heart thumped wildly as I scooted to the middle of the bench seat until my thigh was pressed against his. What I was doing was completely insane, and yet felt completely right. I didn't let strange men touch me. Hell, I'd never even had a boyfriend before, and here I was, ready to strip naked and let this guy ride me hard. He pulled off his glasses and gave me a heated look so full of promises that I nearly climbed him like a tree. Humping him while he drove probably wasn't the best of ideas, though, even if my body was all for it.

"Lift up your dress, princess."

The words were playful, but the tone brooked no argument. The thought of Mr. Sexy telling me what to do warmed me even more. I wiggled my ass and pulled at the skirt until my panties were exposed. The white satin was dripping wet, and I wasn't sure if he'd like it or be horrified. My experience with men was… well; I didn't have it. I'd never even been kissed before, and here I was exposing myself to some stranger. I felt completely wild and out of control. I'd never felt better, more real. This was who I was, a wild woman about to have an orgasm in the front seat of a truck in the middle of the day. The thought of anyone watching just turned me on even more.

His fingers skimmed the inside of my thigh as he nudged my legs apart. As they traced over my panties, he groaned, the sound primitive and hungry.

"Fuck, princess. Is all that for me?"

I couldn't speak, so I just nodded.

"Take the panties off. I want to see what I'm playing with. You want that, don't you, princess? My fingers in your pussy? You want me to make you come?"

"Yes." Oh, God yes!

My cheeks burned as I shimmied out of the panties. I didn't know what to do with them, and Lance took them from me, holding them up to his nose before shoving them in his pocket. I was soaking the seat of his truck, but he didn't seem to care, and I had to wonder just how many times he'd done this. Jealousy spiked inside of me as I thought of him fucking a woman in this truck, making her climax on his fingers. I wanted to be special, but I was too hungry to be picky right now.

His fingers traced my waxed lips, and he shifted in his seat. The bulge in his jeans seemed to have grown even more. He spread my pussy open and licked his lips as he looked at me.

"So pretty and pink. You ever done something like this before, princess? Does it get you off to play around with dirty guys like me?"

"I've never..." My face burned. "I've never done anything before."

The intensity of his gaze burned me. "This is a virgin pussy?"

I nodded.

His finger stroked my clit, and I gave a little cry as my hips bucked toward his hand.

"This is mine, princess. You understand? I'm going to take care of you, take the edge off, but the first cock that's going in this tight little pussy is going to be mine."

I didn't understand the possessive tone of his voice, but I liked it. No, I fucking loved it. My nipples hardened even more, and I pressed myself closer to his hand, wanting more. I needed a release, and I knew only he could give it to me.

"Say it," he demanded. "Tell me this pussy belongs to me."

"My pussy belongs to you."

He stroked my clit, slow swipes that drove me crazy. I dug my nails into his thigh and bit my lip. I felt the tip of his finger press against my entrance and slowly sink inside of me. His thumb teased my clit as his finger stroked in and out of me. I was mindless with need and tried to ride his hand. My dress felt too tight, and I wanted to take it off. A few more strokes and I was coming all over his hand. It was embarrassing how quickly I'd gotten off. He licked my cream from his fingers and shifted in his seat again.

"I could... I could please you now."

Fire burned in his gaze, and I knew he wanted me.

"When we get to my shop, I'm handing your keys to one of the mechanics and then we're going to my office. You're going to strip out of that dress, and you're going to do everything I say. Understand?"

I shivered and nodded. How could I still be so turned on when I'd just had my first orgasm? My thighs were still trembling from the force of my release. It scared me, these crazy things I was feeling for this man, and nothing ever felt more perfect than having his hands on me. If my father knew, he'd blow up and probably lock me away forever. I was a pawn to him, and if I lost my virginity my value would depreciate. I didn't know what it would take to be free of him forever, but for now, I was going to enjoy this moment with Lance. I would take all the pleasure he wanted to give me, and I'd give him just as much back. It was a memory that would have to last a lifetime.

We pulled into the parking lot of a garage and I pulled my dress down. Lance helped me out of the truck, tossed my keys to someone, and dragged me through the shop, down a dark hall, and into a small office. The door slammed shut with such force it rattled on the hinges, and I heard the lock click into place. This was really happening. This insanely gorgeous man was about to make me his. My pussy clenched in anticipation, and I waited to see what he would do.

Chapter Two

Lance

Holy fuck! I had no idea how a piece of ass that fine hadn't been fucked before now, but she was mine, and I was going to enjoy every fucking moment of this. Just the thought of being the first cock she'd ever had was almost enough to make me come in my pants. The moment she'd stepped out of that car, my dick had wanted her. She was sex personified, and it blew my mind that she was completely untouched. Little did she realize that moment she gave me her first orgasm, she became mine.

She was standing in front of me, taking everything in. There was a hint of nervousness to her, but I could tell she wanted this, wanted me. It had been a while since I'd had a woman, but I didn't remember ever being this hard before. I could probably have driven nails with my dick.

"I believe I told you to strip out of that dress when we got in here."

She turned startled eyes toward me and reached for the back of her dress. I heard the zipper rasp, and a moment later, her body was on full display as the garment fell to the floor. Her tits were small, but I couldn't wait to suck them, and her pussy was gleaming from her climax. She tasted sweet, and I wanted more. I was going to make her come so many times she wouldn't remember her name.

"Sit on the edge of the desk, princess, and spread those thighs for me. I want to look at you."

There was crap all over my desk, and I knocked it to the floor so she could sit. Her thighs slowly parted, and her little clit peeked from between her lips. She leaned back on her hands, offering herself to me, despite the blush in her cheeks. I pulled my shirt over my head and let it fall to the floor, her eyes going wide. My chest was tattooed, as were my arms, and I wondered what she thought about the ink. Some women were turned on by it. I'd never given a fuck one way or another, but it mattered this time. I wanted her to want me as much as I wanted her. The moment I'd seen those legs swing out of that little silver coupe, I'd wanted to fuck her.

I stepped between her spread thighs and trailed my hand over her soft skin. She trembled and widened her thighs even more. I'd never seen such a beautiful sight before.

"Unfasten my pants."

It took her a few minutes, but she managed to unbuckle my belt and get my jeans unbuttoned and unzipped. I always went commando, and my cock thrust through the opening as if aiming for her. She reached for me, her hand hesitantly curling around my shaft. Her touch was light, and I wrapped my hand around hers, tightening her grip as I fucked her hand.

"You're not going to fit," she said softly, her eyes wide as she looked at my huge cock.

"Oh, it will fit, princess. All fucking ten inches are going to fit in that sweet little pussy of yours. And you're going to scream for more."

The pulse in her throat leaped. It seemed my princess liked dirty talk.

"Do you know what I'm going to do to you, princess?"

She shook her head.

"First, I'm going to eat this pretty pussy and make you come again. My tongue is going to love every inch of you and lap up every bit of your cream. Then, you're going to suck me off so I can take my time with you. I'm going to use you, fill you with my cum, and you're going to be mine, understand?"

She nodded, but I didn't think she really got it. Once I'd felt her come on my hand, I'd known she was going to belong to me. No doubt there would be obstacles in the way, her being a rich girl and me coming from the other side of the tracks, but I never backed down from anything I wanted. And for some reason, I wanted her. I wanted her passion, her submission, her everything. I wanted to brand her as mine, so she'd never be able to leave. The primitive side of me wanted to mark her with my cum and make sure everyone knew who she belonged to.

The rational part of my brain knew this was insane and completely barbaric, but I didn't much care. All I knew was that I was going to make her mine. I was going to tie her to me so that she could never get away. Just the thought of some other guy putting his hands on her was enough to make me put my fist through a wall.

My hands gripped her thighs as I sank to my knees. Her scent teased my nose and my mouth watered. The lips of her pussy were soft against my tongue, and so very wet. It seemed my princess wanted me real bad. I'd pleasured my share of women during my thirty-two years, and I put every bit of that knowledge to good use. The way she squirmed against me made me want her to ride my face, but I wasn't going to take her on the dirty floor. The moment she'd told me she was a virgin, I should have taken her back to my place, where we'd have a soft bed.

One thing was for sure; I'd never look at my desk the same way again. I'd probably get hard as fuck every time I walked through the door from now on.

But the prize currently perched on my desk was definitely worth the discomfort.

I licked, sucked, and nibbled until she was moaning and squirming for more. Her cream coated my tongue. The more I had of her, the more I wanted. I knew I wouldn't be satisfied until I was balls deep inside of her and she was screaming my name. No way in hell she was leaving this office until I'd claimed her thoroughly. I was going to ruin her for every other man.

My Lady Guinevere made the sweetest noise as she came on my lips and I sucked her clit until tremors wracked her body. Rising to my feet, I gave her a moment to catch her breath. When those blue eyes met mine, I knew that I had her right where I wanted her. That one look said everything I needed to know. She wanted me, needed me, and I was going to make sure she never needed anyone else ever again. I figured access to my cock day and night was a fair trade off for Daddy's money. I only hoped she agreed.

Pre-cum dribbled from the head of my cock, and it pulsed in perfect rhythm with my heartbeat. My Guinevere sank to her knees in front of me. It was hot as fuck seeing her like that, all flushed from her orgasm and submitting to me. Her small, soft hand gripped my cock as she brought those sweet lips closer. Her little tongue flicked out and lapped the tip of my dick before sucking me between those succulent lips.

"That's it, princess." I flexed my hips and sank a little further into her mouth, bumping the back of her throat. I knew she couldn't take all of me, not without gagging, but what she did manage to suck felt fucking fantastic.

She hummed and moaned around my dick, and I knew I wouldn't last.

"That's it, baby. Suck me like a good girl."

Her hips wiggled at my words, and I wondered if she was even wetter than before. Maybe my princess liked being told what to do. She braced a hand on my hip, her nails lightly biting into my skin. That small tick of pain was enough to make my balls draw up. I knew I was going to come at any moment, no matter how much I wished this could last forever.

"I'm gonna come, baby, and you're going to take it all. You understand?"

She hummed again, making my grit my teeth for control.

"Take every fucking drop, princess."

I gripped her hair and took away what little control she had, fucking her mouth with long, deep strokes. She moaned again, and it set me off like a rocket. Spurts of cum bathed her mouth and throat, my hips pumping until every last drop was drained from my balls. Fuck! For a virgin, she sucked cock like a pro.

"Get up here, baby."

I helped her to her feet, slamming my mouth down on hers, our tastes mingling as my tongue thrust between her lips. Her body melted against me as one leg curled around my hip. Just feeling her soft curves pressed against me was enough to make me hard again. I started to wonder if I'd ever get enough of her, or if I'd walk around with a hard-on for the rest of my life.

I lifted her against me and braced her back against the office door. Her legs went around my waist, and my cock brushed against her wet pussy. I didn't want to hurt her, but I knew it was inevitable. At least, that's what I'd heard. I'd never actually taken a virgin before. On my side of town, they were a little rare. Hell, half the girls I'd known ended up pregnant or in prostitution by the age of fifteen. I might not live on the south side of town anymore, but it didn't change the fact I'd grown up there.

"We do this, and you're mine." I stared into her eyes. "You have to tell me what you want, princess."

"I want you." Her fingers caressed my pecs. "I want you to take me, to make me yours."

I claimed her lips as I slowly sank into her warmth, stretching those tight virgin walls. I felt the barrier of her innocence and pushed through. My Guinevere cried out, and I kissed away the tears that trickled down her cheeks. It took every bit of control I possessed to hold still and let her body adjust to my size, but slowly she relaxed. A few slow strokes and she was begging for more.

"Please, Lance. I need…"

"What do you need, princess? You've already got my cock. What else do you want?"

"Harder."

"Deeper?" I growled softly and nipped her jaw. "You want me to fuck you hard and deep? Is that it, princess?"

She nodded and made the sweetest sounds.

I took her like a man possessed, and maybe I was. Nothing had ever felt as incredible as my Guinevere. She was so fucking tight, so wet. So mine! I wasn't even sure if she'd realized I'd taken her bare. I knew I was clean, and since she was an innocent I didn't have to worry about her carrying anything. I'd wanted that skin on skin contact more than anything. It was my first time going bareback, and as fucking fantastic, as it felt, I was never going back. Fuck condoms! Maybe I'd get her pregnant and she'd be mine forever.

Guinevere came apart in my arms, her release coating my cock as I nearly fucked myself into a coma. I knew I was about to come, and I wasn't about to hold back. One thing was for certain though, once wasn't going to be enough.

"Tell me you want my cum, princess. Beg me for it."

She whimpered. "I want your cum."

"You want me to fill this pussy up?'

"God, yes. Yes, Lance!"

It was all the encouragement I needed. I felt like I busted a nut I came so fucking hard, filling her with everything I had. When I pulled out, I watched as some of it dribbled down her thighs. I carried her over to the desk and laid her out on it, spreading her thighs to look at that pretty pussy dripping with our combined releases. I'd never seen anything sexier.

There was a tinge of blood of my cock, the proof of her innocence, and fuck if it didn't just make me hard again. I'd never understood those poor fuckers who were all possessive of their women and shit. I'd enjoyed plenty of women in my time, my first when I was only fourteen, but they'd never been more than a temporary stress reliever, just a way to get off without using my hand. But Lady Guinevere was something else.

"You okay, princess?"

She hummed. "I feel incredible."

I smiled and kissed her stomach. "I'm not done with you yet."

Her eyes widened a little and her lips parted. "There's more?"

"Yeah, princess. There's more. You're not walking out of here until you're covered in my cum and every fucker in a fifty-mile radius knows you're mine."

"Yours. I thought... I thought you only meant for this one time."

I leaned down, caging her between my arms. "When I said your virgin pussy was mine, I meant it. The moment you dropped your panties and let me finger your pussy in my truck, you became mine."

"What... what does that mean, exactly?" She licked her lips. "I have to go home. My father will be mad already that I took off without telling him where I was going."

"Princess, you're a grown-ass woman. It's time to clip that leash your daddy has shoved up your ass." He smirked. "Besides, once I figure out where I put the lube, there's not going to be room for anything in there but my cock."

Her cheeks flushed.

"Oh yeah, baby. Your virgin ass is mine too."

Her pulse fluttered in her throat, and I knew she was just as turned on by the idea as I was. Fuck, she was so damn perfect for me. Minus the rich daddy who was probably going to do everything in his power to keep us apart. I was going to come on her tits, come in her ass, then take that sweet pussy again. I was feeling territorial and knew I was trying to mark her like a fucking dog, but short of branding my name on her ass, I wasn't sure how else to get the point across that she was mine now and not daddy's little girl. I had the urge to throw her over my shoulder and handcuff her to my bed at home until I'd managed to fuck a baby into her.

It wasn't a completely terrible idea. Sure, Daddy Dearest was going to come looking for her, and that fancy ass car of hers probably had some sort of GPS in it, but just because his darling daughter dropped her car off here didn't mean I knew where she was. Right? The more I thought about this plan, the more I liked it. Now I just had to convince the princess this was in her best interest.

Chapter Three

Gwen

My mouth dropped open. "You want me to do what?"

"You're going to move in with me." He ran his hand up and down my thigh making my pussy clench. "I may not live in some big, fancy house, but I can take care of you, princess. You can't tell me you aren't tempted to trade those riches for as many rides on my cock as you want."

"You don't even know my name, and you want me to move in?" I asked slowly. I wasn't sure which was crazier, his idea, or the fact I was tempted. It was a chance to flee my gilded cage. But I would be trading one set of bars for another?

"Sure, I do." He grinned. "It's Lady Guinevere."

I couldn't help but smile. "You're close. It's actually Gwendolyn. My friends and family call me Gwen."

He trailed kisses up my thigh, his beard tickling my skin. "I think I prefer Gwennie or princess."

So did I.

"If you don't come willingly, I'll just throw you over my shoulder and make sure you're nice and secure when we get home. And naked. If you don't have clothes, you can't escape."

"You'd kidnap me?"

"It's only kidnapping if you don't want to be there."

I couldn't fault his logic. But no matter how much I'd love to spend a few days at his house, I knew my father would never allow it. And moving in with him? It was insanity! Wasn't it? People didn't just move in together a few hours after meeting. We hadn't even been properly introduced until now, even if he did know my body better than anyone else. Just because he'd fucked me until I couldn't stand didn't mean I should run off into the sunset with him.

On the other hand, all of those men in suits my daddy had always pushed on me had never done anything for me. There hadn't been so much as a tingle of awareness with any of them, and definitely not with the old lecher who wanted to marry me. He didn't want a wife in the truest sense, though, he just knew he couldn't fuck me if he didn't offer my dad a sweet deal. Thomas Kale III had been eye-fucking me since I turned fifteen, and it hadn't escaped my notice or my father's. The sick part was that I knew my father had been in negotiations with the man ever since about letting Thomas marry me, or at the very least, renting me out. He'd probably wanted a college educated wife, and now that college was off the table I'd sealed my fate. No more waiting, they would strike at any moment, and it wouldn't be marriage on Thomas' mind.

"What is it, princess? You think your daddy intimidates me?"

"It's not just my father. His friend, Thomas Kale III, wants me. I'm pretty sure my father has it all arranged already."

"That old fat guy who lives up on the hill?" Lance asked.

"He's powerful, Lance. One word and he could ruin your business, repossess your cars, foreclose on your home. With just one word he could completely ruin your life and run you out of town."

"Princess, I may live in a nice suburb now, but I'm from the south side of town, and if you think some pompous old man is going to run me off, you'd better think again. He may be powerful because of his money, but his friends aren't the ones who run this town. Mine are."

If he thought that was supposed to comfort me, it didn't exactly work. Just who were his friends that someone like Thomas wasn't a threat to them? I'd seen the man in action and I knew he was ruthless. Was Lance trying to say he was friends with gang members? I was pretty sure we didn't have mafia in our sleepy town, so I couldn't figure out who else he could mean. Was I trading the violence and suppression I'd known my entire life for a new variety? Would I ever truly be free?

I didn't want to live in my world anymore, but I wasn't sure I was ready for Lance's reality either. I'd gotten off on the dirty talk and the demanding tone he'd used with me, and his body was something out of a romance novel, but was that enough to throw everything away and move in with him?

"I mean it, princess. If you say no, I'm hauling your ass back to home and handcuffing your ass to the bed. If you won't listen to reason, I'll just have to give you a reason to stay."

"A reason to stay?"

He gave me a wicked grin and rubbed my belly. "I bet if I fuck a baby into this gorgeous body, you won't want to run off."

Oh, God. His words should have terrified me, made me want to run away, so why was I suddenly very intrigued? I was crazy to even be thinking of running away from my family. It was only a matter of time before my father tracked me to this garage, and he would demand that I return with him. My father was not the type of man who heard the word "no" very often, if ever.

"Lance, you don't understand. They're going to come looking for me. They may even involve the police, and the chief is a good friend of my father's. It's crazy to even think that we could be together. This was incredible, and I wish it could last longer, but it just can't."

He nodded. "Put your dress on."

My shoulders sagged in both relief and disappointment. He was finally going to see reason and I'd be on my way home just as soon as my car was ready. My thighs were sticky and I should have probably cleaned up, but I didn't think Lance would want me to wash his scent off my skin. He seemed a little... possessive.

"Just remember, princess. You brought this on yourself."

He gave me a wicked grin and before I could so much as utter a squeak of protest, he'd thrown me over his shoulder and practically ran to the parking lot. He tossed me onto the seat of an older black sports car then dove behind the wheel before I could even process what had happened. I opened and shut my mouth several times as he peeled out of the parking lot, the back fishtailing as the front tires gripped the road. The engine roared as he sped through town to one of the quieter suburbs.

He pulled into the driveway of a small, white clapboard home with green shutters. It looked like every other home on the street, ordinary and average. I had a hard time picturing Lance living in a home with flowering shrubs out front. He'd said he lived in the suburbs, but I'd figured he meant one of the apartment complexes in town. Lance killed the engine, got out, and slammed his door shut. I looked around, wondering if anyone was watching us. If he carried me into the house the same way he'd carried me to the car, surely someone was going to notice.

The passenger door opened and he hauled me out of the car, flipping across his shoulder and giving my ass a smack before he closed the door and approached the house. I couldn't help but admire the way his jeans molded to his ass and couldn't resist reaching out to grab two handfuls. He let out a throaty chuckle as he opened his house, but he didn't set me down until we reached what I assumed was his bedroom. The bedding was dark and there weren't any curtains at the window.

Lance dropped me onto the bed and immediately began pulling dress off me. I had no idea what he was up to, surely he wasn't *really* going to handcuff me to the bed like he'd said, would he?

"You're mine, princess. I told you this pussy belongs to me now, and I meant it," he said as his fingers teased my slit. "Do I need to keep filling you with my cum until you accept it?"

I swallowed hard. The idea of him fucking me again made me wet and my nipples hardened. His gaze skimmed my body and that grin I was getting used to made another appearance. I watched as he unfastened his jeans and shoved them down his thighs. I had yet to see him completely naked and I felt cheated. I'd been completely on display for him to gawk at and I still hadn't gotten a good look at his body. Everything we don't in his office was a bit of a blur it had happened so fast.

He grabbed my ankle and pulled me to the foot of the bed then flipped me onto my stomach. A smack on my ass made me squeak and clench my thighs. Before today, I never would have guessed that getting spanked would be a turn on. Lance positioned me the way he wanted and without warning, plunged balls deep into my pussy. I was plenty wet and more than ready for him, but I still let out a gasp of surprise.

"You like that, don't you, princess?" he asked, grabbing a handful of my hair and pulling my head back. "You like it when I fuck you like a whore."

He fucked me faster, harder. He went so deep I felt like we were one. The slap of flesh against flesh filled the air along with his grunts and my moans of pleasure. Every thrust pushed me closer and closer to an orgasm. Lance gripped my hair tighter and fucked me like a man possessed. When I let out a scream as my release ripped through me, I heard him give a shout before I felt him come inside of me. If he wanted to get me pregnant, he was well on his way. I wasn't on birth control and we'd had unprotected sex twice now.

He gave me nip on the shoulder and growled. "Mine."

"Yours," I whispered.

He pulled away and there was another smack on my ass. "I won't handcuff you, but I don't want you to leave the house. The backyard is fenced, but it's just chain link, so anyone could see you. If you really want to hide from Daddy Dearest, you'd do better to stay inside. I'm not trying to make you a prisoner, Gwennie, but I'm not letting you go."

"And you think Daddy will be easier to fight off if I'm pregnant?" I asked.

He smirked. "Well, I don't know if he would be easier to fight off, but I sure do like the idea of you carrying my kid. You should feel honored, princess. Lots of women have wanted to be where you are right now. I've even had a few try to trap me over the years. I may not be rich by your standards, but I have a nice home, I own the garage, and I put in a hard day's work. That means something where I come from."

I stood and wrapped my arms around his waist, resting my head against his chest. "If you think I look down on you because you don't live on the hill, I don't. I've never really belonged in that world, even if I was born to it. I've spent most of my life wishing I could escape and have a normal life."

"How old are you, princess?"

"Twenty."

"So you're plenty old enough to make your own decisions then."

I nodded.

"What do you say, Gwennie? Want to make an honest man of me?"

I couldn't help but snicker, and then his words registered. "You want to marry me?"

He tipped my chin up. "Princess, I want to have a family with you. Marriage just seems like the logical step to get there. I want you in my life from here on out. If you don't want to marry me, then I'll wait, but that doesn't mean I'm letting you go."

I had to think about it. If I were married, it would be a little harder for Daddy to get his hands on me. And I had to admit, the idea of puttering around the kitchen, barefoot and pregnant, was pretty amazing. Except for the part where I had no idea how to cook. I had a feeling I'd be watching lots of YouTube videos in the future to figure out how to scramble an egg or make bacon. I didn't even know how to open a can of biscuits.

"You really want to marry me?" I asked.

"I want you to be mine in every sense of the word, princess. And if you want to put a ring on my finger, I'll gladly wear it to show everyone that the hottest woman on earth has agreed to be mine. You never have to worry about me straying, Gwennie. I don't want anyone but you. The moment those legs of yours swung out of that little coupe, I knew I wanted you. And the moment my dick got balls deep inside of you, I knew I was never letting you go."

He was offering me everything I'd ever wanted. A family, a normal life. It would be crazy to turn him down, but I couldn't help but worry about what Daddy and Thomas would do when they found out. I hadn't lied. They would do everything in their power to ruin Lance and his business. It would be selfish of me to take him up on the offer. But I wanted to, so badly.

The thump of his heart was comforting. I had a big decision to make. I could either spend every night for the rest of my life curled up beside my sexy mechanic with that heartbeat in my ear as I fell asleep, or I could run back to Daddy and live a life that I never wanted, either as arm candy for a man old enough to be my grandfather, or rented out to whichever man could pay the most or would influence my father's finances the most. It would be like living in a revolving door, especially if he realized I wasn't a virgin anymore. And if I did end up pregnant with Lance's kid, I had no doubt that Daddy would force me to get an abortion. The thought sickened me.

"You're thinking too hard, princess."

"Let's do it. I want to marry you." I looked up into his eyes. "You're offering me everything I've ever wanted, but all I'm giving you in return is --"

"You. A family. You're giving me just as much in return, Gwennie. Don't worry about your father or Kale, I'll take care of them. It would be an honor to be your husband and the father of your kids. If your father wants a war, I'll give him a war. But I meant what I said, princess, I'm never letting you go."

I pressed my lips to his and opened as his tongue flicked against them. It wasn't a kiss so much as a claiming. Every touch, every kiss, every time we fucked, it was a way for Lance to brand me as his, and I fucking loved it. Who'd have ever guessed I was such a dirty girl? I couldn't help but smile against his lips. In all my life, I'd never felt as happy as I did right now. Maybe I'd fallen a little in love with him the moment I'd seen that swagger heading my way, my heart had certain skipped a few beats. Whatever it was, this feeling that consumed me, I never wanted it to stop.

Lance pulled away and smoothed a thumb across my lower lip. "I'm going to find out what we need to do in order to get a marriage license and how long it takes. Of course, if I didn't think your daddy would be watching the flights and trains, I'd just take you to Vegas to get married."

I smiled. "I've never been to Vegas, but you're right. I'm sure Daddy will be watching for that, once he realizes I'm missing. And if we get married here, he has friends at the courthouse, so I'm sure someone would tell him I applied for a marriage license."

Lance scratched his beard. "Let me make some calls, princess. One way or another, we're getting married. And if that means Vegas, I'll figure out how to get us there. Just need to call in to work and let them know that I'm taking some time off and make sure no one says anything about where you are."

I kissed his cheek. "Then you'd better get busy."

Lance pulled a tee out of his dresser and tossed it to me. "You can wear that for now. You'll have to wear your dress for us to get the hell out of here, but once we get to Vegas, I'm taking you shopping. Not that I have a problem with you running around naked."

Yeah, I was sure he didn't. The man couldn't seem to keep his hands off me, but I felt the same about him. I pulled the shirt over my head and followed him through the house. My stomach growled, reminding me I hadn't eaten in a long time, so I rummaged through his fridge and cabinets in the kitchen to find something to snack on. There was a hunk of cheese and some crackers, so I fixed a plate and sat at the small table. I could hear him in the living room on the phone, but I didn't pay attention to what he was saying. I was too focused on what would happen if my daddy caught me in this house dressed in nothing but Lance's shirt and his cum dripping down my thighs. There would be hell to pay, and that was putting it mildly.

Lance appeared in the doorway and went to the fridge. He pulled out two sodas and gave me one. His fingers curled into my hair and tipped my head back so he could plant a kiss on my lips. Even that small amount of contact was enough to make me want him again, even if I was on the sore side.

"Our flight is leaving in an hour from a private airstrip outside of town. My friends pulled through for me and our flight will not put up any red flags for your family. It turns out the Scarlioni family is in town and since no one can connect either of us to them, we're in the clear."

My brow furrowed. "How do you know them?"

"I don't, but my friends do business with them from time to time. When they explained that true love was on the line, the sappy Italian offered up his jet. Although, I did mention it would thwart Thomas Kale III and some other snooty people, so I'm sure that helped our cause. No one around here likes the people up on the hill -- no offense, princess."

"None taken."

"We should probably shower and dress. As much as I love my cum running down your legs, we don't want to get the seats on the jet sticky."

I pushed my empty plate away, took another swallow of the soda, and stood up. Lance laced our fingers together and led me into the master bathroom. It was small, even smaller than my closet, but I didn't mind since it just meant I'd have to stand closer to him. He started the shower and began stripping out of his clothes, my eyes glued to every move he made. As his body came into view, I ran my fingers over his tattoos and wondered what they all meant. He had a full sleeve and another design across his chest. There were words down his ribs that looked familiar, but I couldn't place them. As he turned to test the water temperature, I saw more ink on his back.

"Like what you see, Gwennie?"

I licked my lips and nodded.

He gave me that playful smirk and dropped his pants, kicking off his shoes before stepping out of the jeans. Seeing him completely naked just made me want to run my hands all over him and explore every inch, but if the jet was taking off in an hour, I knew we didn't have much time. He helped me over the edge of the tub and we washed each other. I'd expected some sexy scented shower gel, but he just had regular soap, and his shampoo and conditioner were a cheap brand that advertised it smelled like an ocean breeze. I was a little surprised, because he didn't seem like the type to use conditioner.

By the time we were finished and dried off, I shimmied back into my dress and heels while he put on a pair of clean jeans and another tee. Before he let me out of the house, he watched the street for a few minutes to make sure nothing looked out of the ordinary, then he rushed me to the car in the driveway. The windows were tinted so I didn't worry about anyone seeing me in his car, but if my dad had tracked my car to Lance's shop then there was a chance people would be looking for his car. I hoped like hell he was doing the speed limit and wouldn't get pulled over. That was the last thing we needed.

The private field came into view and I breathed a sigh of relief as we pulled down the bumpy drive. Lance pulled his car into the large hangar and got out. A man in dress slacks and a tie came over and shook hands with him. I wasn't sure if Lance wanted me to stay put or get out. He threw a smile my way and motioned for me to get out of the car. I shut the car door and walked over to Lance. He reached for my hand, pulling me to his side as he introduced me to the pilot, and then we were boarding the jet.

"Are we leaving the car in here?" I asked.

"If it's in the hangar, people won't notice it. I don't know if your family uses this airfield or not, but this hangar is reserved for certain families, and I doubt yours is on the list. It's the only way I could think to keep them off our trail a while longer. With any luck, they won't be able to find you until you're married and knocked up."

"My dad would just insist on a divorce and an abortion."

His eyes went cold and flat. "If anyone even so much as tries to kill my baby, or take you away from me, I'm going to fucking end them."

A chill skirted down my spine. I'd never seen this side of Lance before. Yes, he'd been demanding and a little arrogant, but in that moment, I had no idea that he would kill anyone who stood in his way. It made me wonder about the kind of upbringing he had, and made me even more curious about those friends of his. For better or worse, I was about to tie my life to his, and despite the fact that this side of Lance scared me a little, I was still all in. I'd been protected all my life, because I was worth something as commodity to be traded, not because I had worth as a person.

Lance sat in one of the seats and pulled me into his lap. His large hand cupped my cheek and his touch was gentle. The look in his eyes stole the breath from my lungs as I saw the promises he'd already given, and maybe a little something extra. I knew he lusted after me, but maybe there was more to it.

"Gwennie, I want to be perfectly clear. You're mine, and I don't say that lightly. When I tell you that you're mine, it means that I will kill anyone who tries to take you away, anyone who tries to harm our family, and if another guy so much as thinks of touching you, I'll cut off his dick." His thumb brushed over my lower lip. "But it also means you own me, heart and soul. Everything of mine is yours. I don't want any hands on this body except yours. I don't want anyone to carry my baby, except you. When I go to bed at night, I want it to be with you wrapped in my arms, and I want to wake the same way. I'm falling for you, princess. No matter what it takes, I will spend the rest of my life worshiping the ground you walk on, and I will give you everything you've ever needed."

I smiled a little. "Does that mean I get your cock whenever I want it?"

He growled a little. "I love it when you talk dirty, princess. Yeah, you can have my cock whenever you want it."

I snuggled into his and traded a heart on his chest. "I'm yours, Lance. I've never wanted anyone, not even once, but I think I'd die if someone took you from me, or me from you. No one has ever made me feel the way you do, and I want to feel that way every day for the rest of my life."

"Love you, princess."

"I love you, too," I murmured as I closed my eyes and listened to his heart's steady thump.

I must have drifted off because the next thing I knew we were landing in Las Vegas. I felt a thrill as I realized it wouldn't be long before Lance was officially mine. It didn't mean my father wouldn't try to break us up, because he would, but it meant that things would be a little harder for him. Whatever came our way, I knew that Lance and I would face it together.

Chapter Four

Lance

The Vipers had really pulled through for me, not only finding me a private jet but also securing a hotel suite and a wedding chapel. I didn't want my bride to get married in the same dress she'd had on that morning. Despite the urgency I felt over making her mine, we did a little shopping before our appointment at the chapel. And not just for wedding attire, but at least a week's worth of clothes as well. She chose a floral strapless number for her wedding dress that hugged her breasts and trim waist and then flared over her sexy as fuck hips. I was already picturing what she'd look like with that dress flipped up and her bent over the bed.

I'd decided to dress for the occasion, since I only intended to get married once, and had on black slacks with a shirt, tie, and vest. No way in hell I was putting on a jacket, unless it was made of leather. Gwennie didn't seem to mind though, if the naughty look in her eyes was any indication. Fuck, if she looked at me like that every time I dressed up, I might have to do it more often. I was sure I could find an occasion for it every now and then.

While she'd been shopping, I'd made a side trip to a specialty shop up the block. The packages were to be delivered to our hotel suite, which we'd already checked into. Gwennie reached for her bags, but I stopped her and instructed the clerk to have them delivered to our room. I made sure to pay a nice tip to ensure it was done quickly. Since I didn't have to pay for the room or the jet, I could splurge a little and pamper my princess. She deserved it.

Her hand trembled in mine as I led the way to the chapel. I knew what we were doing was completely insane, and I was actually a bit surprised she'd agreed to it, but I didn't for one moment regret my decision. Gwennie needed me, and just maybe I needed her too. I'd been with more women than I could count over the years, but it had always been cold and meaningless. I'd been in search of a release and nothing more. With Gwennie, I felt alive and consumed with passion. I knew it would eventually fade and change to something else, something deeper, and I was okay with that. All that mattered was that she was mine.

I felt like a possessive asshole, which really wasn't like me. I'd never given a fuck if a woman was mine or not. Hell, I hadn't even had an official girlfriend before. One night stands had always been my style, and if I ever went back for seconds, I knew other guys had there between rounds. It never bothered me. At all. But the mere thought of another man's hands on Gwennie and I was ready to commit murder. She was unlike any woman I'd ever met, and I meant that in a good way. All I'd ever known, in an intimate sense, were the sluts and whores who hung out with the Vipers and on street corners in my old neighborhood. Most of the girls I grew up with were now working girls, and I didn't mean at a desk job. Unless it was under the desk, on their knees, with their mouths open.

Gwennie would never fit in with my friends, I knew that, and still I held onto her with both hands in a white-knuckled grip. The Vipers would give me hell for marrying someone so prissy and high maintenance, even though she'd been fairly easygoing so far. I wondered how long it would take her to realize that she couldn't live without Daddy's money, regardless of how much cock she got every night. I hoped like hell I was wrong. She was eager and seemed genuine. I was going with my gut this time, and praying I didn't get burned along the way.

Deep down, I had to wonder if she was just picking the lesser of two evils. At least with me, she got multiple orgasms. With her dad, she was likely to be sold like cattle. I wasn't used to feeling self-doubt and it sucked big ass donkey balls. She seemed to like it when I was in charge, making demands of her. I knew she got off on my dirty talk during sex. One thing was for certain, once we said "I do" it would be a lot harder for her to escape me. Despite my doubts, I was going forward with this marriage and then I was going to fuck her into a coma. I hadn't lied to her. I had no plans for us to leave the hotel except maybe to eat and take in a few shows. The moment I'd felt that pussy wrap around my dick, I'd had the insane urge to get her pregnant. Pregnant women couldn't run away, right? Waddle away, maybe.

The chapel wasn't quite as tacky as some that we'd passed along the way. At least there wasn't an Elvis impersonator. Some old granny, probably the officiant's wife, was playing an organ in the corner. Gwennie had a stunning smile on her face and seemed genuinely happy, even though I knew this was probably a far cry from her dream wedding. If we had more time, and didn't have to worry about her fuckwit of a father, then I'd have gladly given her a nicer wedding at home. Maybe we could renew our vows on our one year anniversary or some shit and do things the right way. I wanted her to know that she meant more to me than a quickie wedding.

We said our vows and exchanged rings. When it was time to kiss the bride, I had to hold myself back. If I gave her the kind of kiss I wanted to, she'd end up in the middle of the aisle on her hands and knees with me balls deep inside of her. I wasn't sure she was ready to put on a show just yet, and I wasn't too keen on someone else checking out my new wife. I'd had sex in front of people before, and while I might treat my wife like a two dollar whore in the bedroom, I wasn't about to fuck her in front of strangers. I might have blue balls by the time we reached our hotel suite, but I was going to keep it in my pants until then.

My phone rang and I saw it was the shop. It was odd for them to call so late so I answered, hoping the building hadn't burned to the ground in my absence.

"What's up, Jim?"

"Boss, you know that flashy Mercedes we have right now?"

"What of it?" I asked.

"Some rich guy came by asking about the woman who was driving it. Now, as far as I'm concerned, I didn't see nothin' and I didn't hear nothin' earlier, but he's demanding to know where his daughter is."

Fuck me. If he'd traced the Mercedes, that meant...

"Give me your phone," I barked at my new wife. She gave me a startled glance before pulling it out of her purse and handing it over.

She had twenty missed calls from "Daddy" and another fifteen from "Thomas Kale III." I popped the battery on her phone and pulled her SIM card. It wouldn't surprise me if they had already traced her to Las Vegas, but I wasn't going to make it easy for them to find her. The hotel wasn't registered to her name, but they could easily go from hotel to hotel flashing her picture until they located her. Fuck! Why couldn't anything ever be easy?

"What's wrong?" Gwennie asked.

"Your dad showed up at the shop. If he traced your car, then I'm sure he's traced your phone too."

She paled.

"Jim, if they come nosing around again, tell them you don't remember her. As of now, she's family. We just got married and that's her asshole father. Keep them off our trail as long as you can."

"You got it, boss," Jim said before hanging up.

"Come on, princess. We have a marriage to celebrate. If your father is on his way here, I want to enjoy as much of our honeymoon as we can."

She looked worried, but nodded her agreement. I never had asked for Gwennie's last name. Well, her former last name. But if Daddy lived up on the hill, then he was someone important, as far as our tiny town was concerned. In the big scheme of things though, he could very well be a small fish in a big pond. Just because he had money, didn't mean he had true power.

The Vipers ran our town, even though the rich people on the hill liked to think they did. I wasn't too concerned. Legally, Gwennie was old enough to make her own decisions, and now that she was my wife, her place was by my side. Even the police chief couldn't say otherwise. I just wished there was a way to make everything go away quietly. I didn't want to physically hurt Gwennie's dad, but if I could find something to hold over him, then maybe I could make him leave us alone.

"What's Daddy Dearest's name, princess?"

"Gregory Montcliff."

I froze in the middle of the damn sidewalk. "You're a Montcliff?"

This is when it would have been awesome if our quick Vegas wedding officiant had said our last names during the ceremony, or if I'd paid attention when we'd gotten our license. I'd been going out of my mind for no fucking reason. Not if Montcliff was her dad.

"Is there something wrong with that?"

"No, princess, that means everything is actually pretty damn perfect right now. How much do you know about your daddy's finances?"

She shrugged and gave me a blank look.

"Your daddy's hands are about as dirty as they get. Remember the Scarlioni family I mentioned? The ones who own the jet we're using? The Vipers aren't the only ones in business with them. Your Daddy Dearest is too."

She snorted. "Yeah, right. My dad is in bed with the mob. Have you ever met my father?"

"Don't need to, princess. His name speaks for itself."

She looked doubtful, but she didn't realize this was good news. Montcliff might be in bed with the Scarlionis, but the Vipers did most of the family's dirty work, which made them even more valuable. So if the Vipers asked the Scarlionis to get Montcliff to back the fuck off, then they'd do it. Or they would make an example of him. Wouldn't really hurt my feelings if someone beat the fuck out of him and cut off a finger or two, but I didn't want to upset my wife either. She might not like her father too much, but I doubted she wanted to see him maimed either.

"When we get to our suite, I want you to soak in a nice, hot bath while I make a phone call." I kissed her cheek. "And then we'll celebrate our marriage and put everything else out of our minds until the time comes that we have to deal with it. Sound good?"

She nodded, but I could tell she wanted to ask some questions about her dad.

The suite was everything I'd hoped it would be, and they'd even provided an edible arrangement. All of our bags from our shopping expedition were stacked along the living room wall. I grabbed Gwennie by the hand and led her into the bedroom and attached bath. There were jars of bath salts, some bath oils, and even some bubble bath on the counter. I started the water in the tub and added a little of the oil and a little of the bubbles. After giving her a kiss that I hoped curled her toes, I left her to her bath and went to make my call.

Usually, I only spoke to the Scarlionis through the Vipers, but I did have the contact number for one of the sons. Salvatore Scarlioni. I only hesitated a moment before pushing the call button.

"Who is this?" the Italian barked into the phone.

"Lance Gilbert. We met at a party the Vipers were throwing about a year ago."

"The mechanic."

"Yes." At least he remembered me. That might make things easier.

"What can I do for you, Mr. Gilbert? I'm assuming there's a reason for this call. You've had my number all this time and haven't used it before now."

"I got married today. To Gwendolyn Montcliff."

He let out a whistle. "How did you get the pampered princess away from her daddy? Last I'd heard, he planned to use her to sweeten a few deals he has going. You know I don't agree with pimping your own flesh and blood, but that man isn't above it."

"Her car broke down and I came to the rescue. To make a long story short, we're in Vegas and we just got married. But I think Gregory is going to cause trouble. In fact, he may already be on his way here."

"And you want me to intercept him? To run him off? To make him disappear for good? What precisely do you want to happen?"

All of the above? No. He was Gwennie's dad, even if he was a rotten bastard of the first order.

"I need him to understand that Gwennie is mine now. I don't want him to contact her. I sure as hell don't want him to try taking her from me. He needs to know there will be consequences if he tries."

It was quiet on the other end of the phone for several minutes and I worried I'd overstepped my bounds. Not many guys could make me tremble in my boots, but Salvatore Scarlioni was one of the ones who could. The bastard was ice cold and had a dead look in his eyes. He was a man who got things done, no matter the cost, and it never so much as gave his conscience a twinge. I'd known when I made the call that I wasn't getting out of this unscathed. The question was what would he demand in return? Any price would be worth it. I'd do anything for my princess.

"I'll help you, but you're going to owe me a favor. I don't know yet what it will be, or when. It could be next week or five years from now, but when I call, you will come. Understood?"

"Yes. Whatever it is, I'll do it. I just need to know that my wife is safe."

"Very well. I will extend the protection of the Scarlioni name to your Gwennie, and I'll make sure that Mr. Montcliff understands that you and your business are to remain untouched as well. He's not going to take this well."

"I know. Thank you, Mr. Scarlioni. I appreciate your willingness to help. Whenever you're ready for that favor, call and I'll answer. Although, if I'm balls deep inside my wife, it may go to voicemail. Just sayin'."

Salvatore chuckled. "In that instance, I wouldn't blame you. From what I remember of Gwendolyn Montcliff she's quite fetching. Enjoy your honeymoon, Mr. Gilbert. I'll be in touch."

The dial tone greeted my ear and I hung up the phone. That hadn't been as hard as I'd thought it would, and at least I had peace of mind now. Even if her father was in Vegas this very moment, he wouldn't be looking for us anymore. This might make for awkward family reunions in the Montcliff house, but I would be happy if Gwennie never saw the man again. I wasn't enough of an asshole to tell her she could never visit though. I'd just be worried as fuck until she returned home each time. I wondered if it would be too over the top to install a tracker in her.

I stripped out of my clothes and rummaged through the sacks in the living room. After selecting two of the special items I'd purchased, I went into the bathroom to join my blushing bride. I couldn't help but smile when I saw she'd fallen asleep in the tub, and I knew just the way to wake her up. I set the toys on the floor beside the tub and slowly climbed in, trying not to disturb her. Pulling her legs apart, I settled between her splayed thighs, on my knees, facing her. I picked up one of her surprises and turned it on, a gentle whirring sound filling the air.

With a wicked grin, I stuck the toy beneath the surface of the water and teased the lips of her pussy with it. Gwennie moaned and arched her back a little. God she was sexy as hell. The bubbles lapped against the swells of her breasts and I wished those pretty pink nipples would peek above the surface. I'd bet money they were hard right now.

I teased her clit with the vibrator and watched a rosy hue climb her neck and settled in her cheeks. Her eyes opened to slits and she blinked at me sleepily. I swirled the toy over her clit again and her thighs squeezed me. I knew what she wanted. She wanted my cock, but she wasn't getting it. Not yet anyway. I could tell when she was getting close and I backed off, wanting the moment to last longer. I wanted her every bit as desperate for me as I was for her.

"Please, Lance."

"Please what, princess?"

"Make me come."

"Only if you offer up those gorgeous tits to me. I want to see those pretty nipples when you come."

She moaned and cupped her breasts, lifting them out of the water. Droplets dripped from the points of her hard nipples and I ached to lick them. This wasn't about me though, right now was about Gwennie. I watched as she came apart, crying out her release. My cock was so fucking hard I was in agony, but it was the sweetest kind of torture.

I turned off the toy and tossed it aside before gathering her in my arms. Her legs slipped around my waist and my dick brushed against her slit. He was a hungry bastard and wanted in. She wiggled against me and made little frustrated huffing sounds. I smiled as I realized she was trying to squirm until my dick slipped inside of her. All she had to do was ask.

"You know I'll give you anything you want, right, princess? As long as it's within my power to give it to you."

"Anything?" she asked.

I nodded.

She leaned closer and nipped my ear, making my cock jerk. "Then put that big dick inside of me and fuck me until you fill me with your cum."

Holy shit! Hearing those dirty words come out of such a pristine woman was almost enough to make me come on the spot. I gripped her waist and lifted her up, then eased her down on my cock. She moaned and tipped her head back as I filled her. I helped her ride me, the water sloshing over the side of the tub. I didn't care if we flooded the whole damn bathroom as long as she kept squeezing my dick like that.

I was too far gone to last very long, but I refused to come before she did. My thumb tapped her clit until she was screaming my name and coating my dick with her cream, and then I let loose. That hadn't quite been what I'd thought would happen for our first time as husband and wife, but Gwennie didn't seem to be complaining. I'd thought I would ravage her in a bed and we'd go all night long, but I could see the shadows under her eyes and I realized she needed sleep more than she needed my cock all night long.

I lifted her off my cock and she sank into the water again. She looked flushed and well pleasured. There was still the matter of the toy sitting beside the tub, the one I hadn't used yet.

"Are you up for one more thing, princess? And then I'll let you get some sleep."

She gave me a drowsy smile. "Of course."

"Hands and knees, princess."

The water sloshed as she rolled onto her hands and knees, her ass rising out of the water. I reached for the toy and stuck it under the water before she could see it. I hadn't thought to grab lube out of the sack and I hoped the bath oils would coat it enough for what I had in mind. Her skin was slippery from the oils and bubbles as I ran my hand over her ass cheek. I parted those sweet cheeks and leaned forward to tease her with my tongue, flicking it against the tightest hole I was ever going to put my dick in. She gasped, but she didn't pull away. I played with her alternating between my tongue and my fingers, until I thought she was relaxed enough to accept the butt plug I'd bought. She was going to wear it all night, and come morning, I was going to take her in the one place that remained untouched.

I eased the toy inside of her and gave it a flick with my finger when it was all the way in. Gwennie wiggled her hips, but she didn't utter a word of protest.

"Come on, princess. Let's get dried off and go to bed."

"You're... you're leaving it in there?" she asked.

"All night, princess. And then in the morning, we're going to have some fun."

Goose bumps rose along her back, but I could tell she was turned on. She might not have admitted it, but she wanted me to take her there. Her body was so damn responsive I couldn't wait to see what morning would bring.

"Take it out," she said.

"Princess, did you forget that when you stripped in my office you agreed to do as I said?"

"I don't want to wait, Lance. I want you to take me now."

"Gwennie, you're tired and I don't have lube in here."

"Then get some."

She really wanted this right here and now? It was our wedding night, so it would be a dick move to deny her, but I wasn't sure she was ready. Yeah, I'd wanted to be balls deep in her ass since the moment she stripped in my office, but I could be a patient guy. Moderately patient.

"Please, Lance. Don't make me beg. I... I need this."

I got out of the tub and dripped water all the way to the living room. I grabbed the lube out of the sack from the specialty shop and went back into the bathroom. She was still on her hands and knees, waiting. But no, if we were going to do this, it wasn't going to be a quick fuck in the tub. We were going to do this the right way.

"Get out of the tub, Gwennie. We're taking this to the bedroom. If you really want me that way, it's not going to be fast."

I helped her out of the tub and dried both of us off. She sauntered into the bedroom and climbed onto the bed, resuming her position on all fours. If we were going to do this, I needed to get some control over myself. I'd already come once, but just the thought of taking her ass had me fucking hard as a rock. I needed to take the edge off so I didn't pound her like an animal. She deserved better than that.

This wasn't some dirty, quick fuck from a one-night stand. This was my wife. I smiled just thinking the word "wife."

"Princess, are you sure about this? Because I'm going to take my time. And I'm not just going to tap that ass of yours either. I'm going to fill every hole you've got, mark you as mine as thoroughly as I can."

She shivered, but the heated look in her eyes told me everything I needed to know.

I walked around to the other side of the bed, dropping the lube onto the mattress. My fingers tunneled through her hair and tipped her head back so I look into those beautiful blue eyes. She looked hungry, and needy as hell.

"Open up, princess. You're going to suck my cock. I'm going to fuck this sweet mouth of yours until I come down your throat, and you're going to swallow every drop, aren't you?"

She nodded eagerly and opened her mouth.

Those pouty lips wrapped around my dick as I sank into heaven. Her tongue was soft and wet against my shaft. Even if she couldn't take all of me, it was enough to both torment and tease me. She made sexy little moans, her mouth humming around my cock. I could fuck her like this for hours, it felt so damn good. She sucked me like a pro and swirled her tongue over the tip of my dick, flicking the hole with just the right amount of pressure. God, I wished I could come over and over and over again. I'd fuck her all night long in every way imaginable, and then do it all over again tomorrow. If I could, I'd stay locked in this room with her for weeks. I knew the things I did to her made her feel dirty, but she liked it. She liked it when I took charge and told her what to do.

"Relax your jaw, princess. I'm going to fuck you until I come."

Her tongue continued to tease me as I fucked her mouth with long, slow strokes. Sweat rolled down my spine as I fought for control. My balls drew up and I groaned as I quickened my pace. Watching my dick disappear between her lips just made me hotter. She looked like an angel, so prim and proper, letting the bad boy do naughty things to her. *Oh fuck!*

I came down her throat and gave a few more thrusts before pulling out of her mouth. She licked her lips and gave me a sultry look that instantly had my dick hard again. For someone who had been a virgin less than twenty-four hours ago, she'd certainly learned the art of seduction rather quickly.

"We're not done yet, princess. Are you ready for more?"

"Yes." She licked her lips again and it made me want to smear them with my cum. Jesus. If I didn't get myself under control, I was going to take her like a fucking beast, whether she was ready or not.

I picked up the lube and climbed onto the bed behind her. I wanted her ready when it came time for the next step, so I removed the butt plug long enough to lube her ass really well, then I stuck the toy back in. She groaned and wiggled her ass at me so I gave it a playful smack. I watched as her pussy clenched and I grinned. My princess liked things a little rough. If she wanted her ass smacked, I'd be glad to do it again. Preferably with my dick inside of her.

I tossed the lube aside and pushed her head down toward the mattress. Her pussy was so wet and swollen with need. Her little clit peeked between her lips and I leaned down to flick it with my tongue. Oh yeah, I was going to have some fun with my princess tonight. She'd be sore tomorrow, but it would just serve to remind her that she was mine. Every step she took, she'd be thinking about me.

I sucked and licked her pretty pussy until she was creaming my tongue, and even then I didn't let up. I teased her until she was on the edge again, and only then did I pull away, leaving her wanting more. My dick jerked just thinking about how tight and wet she was. Without giving her any warning, I thrust into her hard and fast, filling that sweet pussy. I pulled out and stared at my cock, shiny with her juices, before I sank into her once more. I loved watching her accept my cock, sliding into her with ease. She gripped me tight, her pussy clenching on my dick with every thrust.

Bracing a hand on the bed, I leaned over her and drove into her again and again. I fucked her like a man possessed, and maybe I was. When she came again, I let go, giving her everything I had, all ten inches as fast and hard as I could. No matter how hard I fucked her, I just couldn't get deep enough. My balls were heavy and I felt that familiar tingle in my spine that told me I was close to coming. Gripping her hips, I took her hard, fast, and deep.

"You like that, don't you, princess?"

"Yes," she cried out.

"You like it when I take this pussy hard. You like it when I fuck you deep."

"More," she begged.

"You want my cum? You want your pussy dripping with it?"

She cried out again, my words triggering another orgasm, and I sank into her deep, filling her up until it was dripping down her thighs. When I pulled out, her lips were coated with my cum and I smiled smugly. I was marking my territory, and damned if I didn't love it. If I'd known fucking without a condom felt so damn good, I would have gotten a wife sooner. Except then I wouldn't have had my Gwennie, and she was fucking perfect for me.

I leaned down and nipped her ass cheek. "Are you ready for what comes next, Gwennie? Are you ready for my cock in your ass?"

The ass in question clenched the toy tighter and I groaned. I could come just watching her. One of these days, I was going to buy her a dildo and jack off while I watched her get herself off, and then I'd come all over her tits. A plastic dick was the closest she would ever get to having a cock that wasn't mine.

I eased the butt plug from between her cheeks and lubed her up again. My cock was still wet from our combined releases. I pressed the head against the tight ring of muscle and gently pushed until I popped through. She gasped and her body tensed. I was a lot bigger than the toy, but I knew she could take me. Sweat coated my skin as I used shallow thrusts until I managed to get all the way inside of her.

"How do you feel, princess?"

"Full and empty at the same time."

"Is that sweet pussy feeling neglected?"

She nodded. I might have to look into that dildo idea. Just the thought of stuffing her with two dicks was enough to make my cock swell.

"Hold on tight, Gwennie. I don't know how gentle I can be."

She whimpered a little and fisted the covers.

Watching her ass stretch tight around my cock was such a fucking turn on. I tried to be easy, to be gentle, but she felt so damn good my control slipped. I took her harder and faster, my balls slapping her pussy with every thrust. I wanted her to come with me so I toyed with her clit until she was pressing back against me, begging for my dick.

"You want me to pound this ass?" I asked, giving her ass cheek a slap.

She squeaked and tensed.

"Do you, princess?"

"Yes. Don't hold back, Lance."

It was all the encouragement I needed. I pounded into her until both of us found our release. I pulled back, withdrawing my cock, and watched as my cum leaked from her ass. Her pussy was still coated and my inner caveman roared his approval. Fuck if seeing her like that didn't make me want to take her again, but I knew she needed a break.

"Come on, princess. Let's get cleaned up and get some sleep."

I helped her off the bed and we got into the shower. It was hard not taking her against the shower wall, but I managed to hold myself back. I was insatiable where she was concerned. Was it too much to hope it would always be like this with us?

I fell asleep that night with her cuddled in my arms. It was the first time I'd had a woman stay longer than a few hours in my bed. Gwennie felt right, curled against me. If every night was like this one, I would die a happy man.

Chapter Five

Gwen

Sunlight streamed through the bedroom windows as I struggled to open my eyes. The blinding light made me wince as I shifted in the bed, Lance's arm weighing me down. There was a pounding coming from the living room and I realized someone was at the door. I slid my hand up Lance's arm and jostled him a little, but he mumbled in his sleep and rolled over. Looked like it was up to me to answer the door. I slid out of bed and grabbed one of the complimentary robes, fastening the sash around my waist as I walked into the living room. The door rattled on the hinges from the force of the pounding and I wondered how long the person had been knocking. For such determination, it must have been important.

Standing on tiptoe, I peered through the peephole and my breath froze in my lungs. With a shaky hand, I undid the security lock on the door and opened it, to stare at my father in shock and horror. He'd found me, and I could only imagine what he would do to me now. I'd ruined all his plans.

"Gwendolyn, would you care to explain why I received a call from Salvatore Scarlioni informing me that my only daughter was married and was to remain out of my reach? What lies have you been spreading about me?"

He nearly knocked me off my feet as he barreled into the room. I let the door close behind him and glanced toward the bedroom. It seemed my husband was sleeping the sleep of the dead.

"Daddy, you shouldn't be here. I'm a grown woman and I can make my own decisions. Lance is good for me."

"You met him and married him all in one day! Do you know the life you could have had as Kale's wife?"

I set my jaw. "Yes, the life of a dutiful slave. And if you think I wanted that fat old man to touch me, then you're delusional. My husband is handsome and sexy, and he's stronger than either you or Kale. Lance may not be rich by your standards, but I will be far happier with him than in the gilded cage you put me in."

"A cage?" My father's face turned purple. "Maybe if I'd had you in a cage you wouldn't have whored yourself out to the first guy who came along."

"Only to the men you wanted to seduce into business, right, Daddy?" I sneered at him. "I knew all about your plans. You were going to sell me to Kale and if that didn't turn out, you were going to use me to turn a profit. You disgust me and I never want to see you again."

A hand settled on my waist and I looked up into Lance's eyes, the pride showing in them stole my breath. He leaned down and pressed a kiss to my neck before facing my father.

"I believe my wife has told you to go fuck yourself. I also know you were told to stay away from her. I'm sure Salvatore will be interested in hearing of your disobedience." Lance gave Daddy a chilling smile. "You know how much he hates to be disobeyed."

My father paled and his hand trembled a little.

"Do you see the kind of monster you married?" Daddy demanded.

"The kind who looks out for me," I replied. "I'm sorry, Daddy. You changed after Momma was gone, and not for the better. You're a cold, heartless man, and

I don't want anything to do with you. Until you can remain civil, I want you to stay away from us. And if we have kids, you won't be welcome to see them."

He drew back as if I'd physically attacked him.

"You'd keep me from my grandchildren? Even knowing what I could do for them?"

"Your gifts always come with strings attached. They don't need that in their lives. Unconditional love is all my children will know, and I'm not sure you know how to give it." I leaned against Lance. "Please leave. If you ever change, I'll agree to meet with you, but it will be on my terms."

"And you bet your ass I'll be there," Lance said. "Gwennie is mine now. You'd do well to remember that."

My father looked defeated as he slunk out of the hotel room, his tail between his legs. It seemed my husband was more badass than I'd realized, and maybe I was too. I'd never stood up for myself before, but Lance was showing me a side of myself I'd never realized was there, just simmering beneath the surface.

"I'm proud of you," Lance said, kissing my cheek. "Let's order breakfast and then we'll discuss when you want to return home, now that we don't have to worry about Daddy Dearest."

"I know this is supposed to be our honeymoon, but I think I'd like to go home, Lance. I want to put my stamp on your house, if that's okay, and try to figure out what I'm going to do with my life now."

"You can do anything you want, princess. You said you dropped out of college because you didn't want to study business. Is there something you did want to study?" he asked.

I shrugged. "I never really thought about it because I was never given any choice in what became of my life."

"What makes you happy, princess?"

"You."

He gave me that sexy grin. "Besides me and the monster cock."

"When I was little, I used to paint. I always enjoyed it and my tutors said I was quite good. I haven't touched a brush in years though. What if I don't have talent at all? What if it looks like an elephant painted it?"

"Then you'll try something else. I'll make sure the jet is ready to leave within the hour and we'll head home. And the first stop we're going to make is to the craft store for you to get as many paints and canvases as you wish. You can set up one of the spare rooms as an art studio until I can come up with something better. If it's your true passion, I'll build one of those pod things in the backyard for you."

I threw my arms around his neck and kissed him until my toes curled.

"Have I told you that you're the best husband ever?" I whispered against his lips.

"How about you show me instead?"

I kissed him again. "You make those flight arrangements and I'll be waiting in the bedroom for you."

Lance smacked my ass as I walked away and I couldn't stop smiling. He acted like a caveman sometimes, but I loved every moment of it. I loved the dirty talk, the way he commanded me to do things. I'd never controlled anything in my life, so it wasn't hard to hand myself over to him, especially when I knew it would only bring pleasure.

I remembered his words at the garage. He'd talked about fucking a baby into me, and even though my father wasn't an issue anymore, I couldn't think of anything I'd like more. With any luck, by the time we got home, I'd already be carrying our first child, even if it meant we fucked like rabbits all the way there. For all I knew, I was already pregnant, but I knew I couldn't take a test this soon.

The robe dropped to the floor and I crawled across the middle of the bed, making sure my ass would be the first thing he saw when he walked through the door. We had yet to make love slowly, but I seemed to like it hard, fast, and dirty, and Lance was more than happy to give it to me. If I didn't know better, I'd swear he had a magic dick. He'd turned me into a wanton whore, but I knew I was his and only his. The possessive glint in his eyes turned me on. I considered myself a modern woman, and I wasn't sure I'd follow any barked orders outside of sex, but I'd be happy to drop to my knees anytime he wanted.

A sharp slap made my right butt cheek sting and I gasped. Sneaky bastard. I hadn't even heard him come in. The sound of his zipper rasping and his pants hitting the floor was enough to make goose bumps spread along my back. I never knew what to expect with Lance, but I knew it would be good. Really, really good. The man was a god when it came to making me scream his name and I wasn't sure I'd turn him away even if we were in the middle of a packed restaurant and he decided to fuck me over the table. I could tell by the way he watched me that he'd never invite someone into our bed, but I wasn't sure how he felt about exhibitionism. It would be interesting to find out. I wondered just how far I could push him in public before he broke.

"Is my naughty wife ready for me?" he asked, his hand slapping my ass again. "Mmm. Your skin pinks so nicely."

"I'm always ready for you. I've been ready since you stepped out of that tow truck and gave me that sexy smile."

He nipped my ass. "You think my smile is sexy, huh?"

"Everything about you is sexy."

His fingers skimmed my slit and I pushed back, wanting more. I didn't care what he did to me, as long as he did it soon. I was aching for him. My nipples were hard enough to cut glass and I could feel my pulse pounding in my clit. He placed his palms on the inside of my thighs and spread my legs further. The flick of his tongue against my pussy was enough to make me pant for more. He alternated between soft and firm strokes as he teased me mercilessly. Lance lifted me off the bed as he buried his face between my legs. I wanted to come so badly, but it was just out of reach.

"My clit," I begged. "Please play with my clit."

He chuckled against me, the vibration making my channel clench. He sucked and licked my clit until I saw stars and came so hard I couldn't breathe. I dropped back down onto the bed and felt his cock at my entrance a moment before he thrust deep. Crying out in pleasure, I gripped his shaft tight as he began fucking me like a man possessed. He took me hard, fast, and deep, just the way I liked it. His hand smacked my ass several times but he never broke stride as he rode me to completion, both of us coming at the same time. I felt the splash of his cum inside of me and I wanted more. I wanted him to fill me up until I couldn't hold anymore, and then I wanted to do it again. I didn't care if I was sore or couldn't walk for the rest of the week. I wanted his baby, and I was going to get one.

"We need to be at the airstrip in two hours."

I rolled over and smiled what I hoped was a seductive smile. "Good. Then we have time to play some more. I want you to fuck me until I can't walk."

"Oh, princess. I can do that."

"But…" I held up a finger. "I want you to fuck my pussy until I can't hold any more cum, and then I want you to fuck my ass."

He arched a brow and studied me.

"You promised you were going to fuck a baby into me." I pouted. "Were you lying to me?"

It seemed he liked the idea of getting me pregnant, if the massive cock standing at attention was any clue. Lance grabbed my ankle, pulled my ass to the edge of the bed, and slid home once more. By the time we had to check out and leave, I could barely walk, but I had the happiest smile on my face.

Epilogue

Lance

Three weeks of wedded bliss and I could barely concentrate on my work. I'd screwed up twice in the shop and Jim had shooed me into the office, not that I was in good enough shape to do payroll either. Especially since I couldn't look at my desk without thinking about fucking Gwennie on it. Maybe having her strip in my office hadn't been such a great idea. Or the dozen times she'd come by since then. We'd been fucking like rabbits since day one, trying for a baby. I was starting to think maybe we were just trying too hard.

I stared at the clock another fifteen minutes before deciding to just say screw it and head home. I asked Jim to lock up and headed out to my car. Fuck. If we did have a baby, we'd have to take Gwennie's Mercedes for family outings, since it was safer than my car. Might be time to invest in a family SUV or something. The maintenance on a nice Chevy or Dodge would sure as hell be cheaper. I wasn't sure how attached Gwennie was to her car, but we might have to talk about selling it. The damn thing had broken twice since the day she ran out of gas, and I wasn't sure it would ever run right again. Not without a new engine, new fuel system, and a host of other things. Might as well get a new car.

When I pulled into the driveway at home, I noticed her car wasn't there. She hadn't mentioned going anywhere, but I didn't exactly keep her on a leash. If she wanted to drive around town, she was more than welcome to. I just hoped she hadn't gone to work to surprise me. Whistling as I entered the house, I turned off the alarm and pulled off my clothes as I headed to the master bath. Even if I hadn't done a lot of work, I'd still gotten more grease on me than the cars I'd worked on, and I didn't like marring my princess's skin with motor oil.

Just thinking of her naked and willing was enough to make my cock hard, but I willed the beast into submission. I hadn't jacked off since the day I found Gwennie in the middle of the road, and I didn't plan to start now. I had a wife who was more than willing to take care of any urges I had. Besides, if I came in the shower, she'd probably give me that stare that secretly scared me and complain that I was slushing our baby down the drain. I got that same look when I wanted to come in her mouth or her ass since she'd decided she definitely wanted a baby. The woman was killing me, but I was going to give in to her... until she was pregnant, then all bets were off. We were going to have a fuck fest when that happened.

I got out and dried off, stepping on something I hadn't noticed on the floor earlier. It was the cardboard box of a pregnancy test. My heart was heavy. She'd taken four in the last few weeks and cried every time it was negative, which probably explained the missing car. She was probably out doing a little retail therapy.

Against my wishes, her father still put money into her account. Not as much as she'd gotten before, but every Friday like clockwork, five hundred dollars would show up in her checking account. I'd confronted him and had gotten the shock of a lifetime. He'd told me that while he might be a bastard and hadn't treated his daughter right, he wasn't going to have her suffer on a mechanic's salary either. Little did he realize that I did pretty well. Maybe not millionaire well, but we could live comfortably.

I strolled into the living room with a pair of athletic pants on, my bare feet slapping against the wood floor, when I heard her car pull in. Peering through the blinds, I tried to gauge her mood. She wasn't smiling, but she didn't seem to be bawling her eyes out either. I opened the door and helped her carry her stuff in. She gave me a kiss on the cheek before snatching one of the bags from me.

"That's a surprise." She smiled. "Close your eyes."

I humored her and closed my eyes, even if I didn't like the thought of her buying me a present with her daddy's money. The bag rustled and she told me to open my eyes. It took me a moment to realize was I was looking at and what it meant. I fingered the teddy bear and stared at her, hoping I wasn't wrong.

"You're pregnant?"

She nodded, squealed, and threw her arms around me. "Do you know what this means?"

Oh, yeah. I knew exactly what it meant.

I slapped her ass. "It means this ass is mine and the next time your mouth is open it had better be to suck my cock."

Her gaze heated. Gwennie tossed the bear onto the couch and sauntered toward the bedroom, pausing in the door.

"Well, are you going to come fuck me or stare at me?" she asked.

"Oh, princess. I'm going to fuck you all night long in every way I can imagine. I hope you're ready to get ridden hard."

Gwennie dropped her jeans and wiggled her thong-clad ass at me.

"Then come get it… Daddy."

Fuck me! I might never be a millionaire like Daddy Dearest, but fuck if I didn't feel like the king of the world right then. I had the hottest woman in the world as my wife, and we were having a baby. Everything was abso-fucking-lutely perfect.

I gave her a little growl as I chased her into the bedroom. I had a feeling both of us would be walking funny come morning.

Harley Wylde

Harley Wylde is the international bestselling author of the Dixie Reapers MC, Reckless Kings MC, Devil's Boneyard MC, Devil's Fury MC, and Hades Abyss MC series.

When Harley's writing, her motto is the hotter the better -- off-the-charts sex, commanding men, and the women who can't deny them. If you want men who talk dirty, are sexy as hell, and take what they want, then you've come to the right place. She doesn't shy away from the dangers and nastiness in the world, bringing those realities to the pages of her books, but always gives her characters a happily-ever-after and makes sure the bad guys get what they deserve.

The times Harley isn't writing, she's thinking up naughty things to do to her husband, drinking copious amounts of Starbucks, and reading. She loves to read and devours a book a day, sometimes more. She's also fond of TV shows and movies from the 1980s, as well as paranormal shows from the 1990s to today, even though she'd much rather be reading or writing.

You can find out more about Harley or enter her monthly giveaway on her website. Be sure to join her newsletter while you're there to learn more about discounts, signing events, and other goodies!

Harley at Changeling: changelingpress.com/harley-wylde-a-196

Changeling Press E-Books

More Sci-Fi, Fantasy, Paranormal, and BDSM adventures available in e-book format for immediate download at ChangelingPress.com -- Werewolves, Vampires, Dragons, Shapeshifters and more -- Erotic Tales from the edge of your imagination.

What are E-Books?

E-books, or electronic books, are books designed to be read in digital format -- on your desktop or laptop computer, notebook, tablet, Smart Phone, or any electronic e-book reader.

Where can I get Changeling Press E-Books?

Changeling Press e-books are available at ChangelingPress.com, Amazon, Apple Books, Barnes & Noble, and Kobo/Walmart.

ChangelingPress.com

Printed in Great Britain
by Amazon